The Diary of a Man of Fifty

The Diary of
a Man of Fifty

Henry James

ET REMOTISSIMA PROPE

Hesperus Classics

Hesperus Classics
Published by Hesperus Press Limited
4 Rickett Street, London sw6 1ru
www.hesperuspress.com

'The Diary of a Man of Fifty' first published in *Harper's New Monthly Magazine*, 1879;
'A Bundle of Letters' first published in *Parisian*, 1879;
'The Point of View' first published in *Century Magazine*, 1882
First published by Hesperus Press Limited, 2008

Foreword © David Lodge, 2008

Designed and typeset by Fraser Muggeridge studio
Printed in Jordan by the Jordan National Press

ISBN: 978-1-84391-178-4

CONTENTS

'The Diary of a Man of Fifty', first published in 1879, is not a well-known story, even among devoted readers of Henry James. It is not available in any of the several selections of his shorter fiction currently in print, which is one reason to be grateful to Hesperus Press for reprinting it. David Garnett included it in his selection, *Fourteen Stories* (1946) which he said contained those 'which I like the most and believe to be the best introduction to reading James at all'. His high regard for this one has not been widely shared by later critics, though Fred Kaplan praised it as 'a fully realised, brilliant story about anxiety, commitment and marriage in *Henry James: the Imagination of Genius* (1992).

I must admit to having reservations about the phrase 'fully realised' in that description, but there is no doubt that 'The Diary' (as I shall refer to it henceforth) is a very interesting story, for several reasons. It is one of the very few of James' numerous stories and tales (well over a hundred in total) to be written in a diary or journal form. I have been able to identify only three others, two of them very early – 'A Landscape Painter' (1866), and 'A Light Man' (1869) – the third one, 'The Impressions of a Cousin' being published a few years after 'The Diary' in 1883. The diary form differs from a retrospective first person narrative, which James used on many occasions, in that the narrator is not describing, with the wisdom of hindsight, an action which is already concluded, but reporting on a day-to-day sequence of events, moving uncertainly into an unknown future, as we do ourselves in real life. This method is well suited to dramatise a mental process of speculation, interpretation, and discovery, which is the essential action of 'The Diary'. (The reader may wish to postpone reading the rest of this introduction until after perusing the story.)

A 52-year-old English general comes back from long service in India and revisits the city of Florence, where twenty-seven years earlier he came under the spell of a beautiful widow, the Countess Salvi, competing for her attention with a little court of Italian admirers. Eventually, having come to the conclusion that she was a heartless coquette who only wanted 'a rich, susceptible, credulous, convenient young Englishman established near her *en permanence*', he broke off the connection and went to India; but when – still a bachelor – he returns to Florence, it revives vivid memories, pleasant and painful. He knows that the Countess Salvi is dead but learns that her daughter resides in the same palazzo under the name of Salvi-Scarabelli, and he calls on her. She too is a bewitching widow, and surrounded by a little court of admirers – among them a young Englishman, Stanmer, in whom the General finds an eerie resemblance to his own youthful self. The General is fascinated, indeed obsessed, with the 'analogy' he perceives between the young man's relationship with the daughter and his own in time past with the mother. As James put it in his notebook when he first conceived the story, their situations 'correspond at all points… so that at last he determines to warn him and open his eyes.' The General reveals to Stanmer that what impelled him to break off his relationship with the mother was discovering that she had admitted to her intimate circle the man who had killed her husband in a duel. 'It was a tremendous escape! I had been ready to marry the woman who was capable of that!' His disillusionment was completed when he heard later that she had married the duellist. He is convinced that her daughter has the same amoral character beneath her beauty and elegant manners, and does his best to turn Stanmer against her.

That was as far as James sketched the story in his notebook. In working it out he made the General into one of his interestingly unreliable narrators, a man who insists on interpreting others' behaviour within the rigid frame of his own preconceptions, while missing the truth about himself. Stanmer's insistence on the daughter's virtue has no effect on him; nor does her own observation (for she is well aware of the trouble the General is causing): 'I think you are a little crazy…You have, at any rate, what we call a fixed idea.' Eventually the General gives up the struggle and leaves Florence: 'It is the same story; but why, a quarter of a century later, should it have the same *dénouement*? Let him make his own *dénouement*.' And so the young man does – but it is not the one the older man predicted. Soon he hears that Stanmer has married his Countess and, a few months later, meets him in London, obviously happy in his marriage. 'Depend upon it you were wrong!' Stanmer declares. The General accepts his word and hopes the Countess has forgiven him. 'I was not alluding to my wife,' says the young man, 'I was thinking of your own story.'

This remark hits the man of fifty with the force of a thunderbolt. Is it possible that he was mistaken about the Countess Salvi? That she was really a woman of integrity in need of a protector – and that he deprived both her and himself of the possibility of happiness by turning his back on her because she offended his stiff-necked ideas of propriety? We leave the General turning over these questions in his mind, fearing more and more that the answers must be 'yes'. It is a neat reversal which reverberates back through the pages of his diary and throws a new light on his cherished 'analogy'.

'Don't you think you rather overdo the analogy?' Stanmer asks the General at one point, and we may think that James himself overdid the symmetry between the two generations to make his character's obsession explicable. It is a highly stylised story, which requires from the reader a generous suspension of disbelief in places – for example the complicated intrigue surrounding the duel in which the Count Salvi was killed. But 'The Diary' anticipates one of James's greatest stories, written much later, 'The Beast in the Jungle', about a man who spends his whole vacant life in expectation that something very important will one day happen to him, confiding this obsession to a woman friend, only to discover when she dies that what he had lacked was the capacity to recognise and return the love she was offering him. The moment comes when he visits her grave and sees a man at the tomb of another woman, obviously in the grip of passionate grief, and realises that 'He had seen *outside* of his life, not learned it within, the way a woman was mourned when she had been loved for herself.' There is a strikingly similar observation in 'The Diary' when Stanmer defends his commitment to his beloved by saying, 'Things that involve a risk are like the Christian faith; they must be seen from the inside.'

Why did Henry James, at the age of thirty-six, think up a story of a man of fifty who comes painfully to question whether he was right to reject the possibility of a woman's love half a lifetime ago? Was he brooding on some opportunity of the same kind in his own life, and wondering if he would regret not having taken it? We know that it was in the late 1870s that James came to the firm conclusion, to the dismay of his parents, that he would never marry. Fred Kaplan links 'The Diary' with another story about crossed purposes and missed opportunities in regard to marriage written the year before – 'Longstaff's Marriage' – and observes, 'Whatever the emotional sources of James' own disinclination to marry, these stories both reveal and disguise a pervasive anxiety about marriage.' The same anxiety about emotional commitment afflicts other protagonists of the stories of this period – Longmore in 'Madame de Mauves', for instance, and Winterbourne in 'Daisy Miller'. We might speculate that the anxiety had its source in James' increasing awareness of his own ambivalent sexuality: though he enjoyed the company of women and appreciated female beauty, he seems not to have desired them, while he was inhibited by temperament and principle from acting out any desires he had for his own sex (at least, that is my opinion – others think differently). He dramatised this anxiety in stories about the emotional entanglement of diffident, convention-bound young men with women of problematical moral character – usually older and sexually experienced women. He rationalised his own decision to remain a celibate bachelor as a dedication to his artistic vocation, but with a lingering worry that by so doing he was cutting himself off from the vital core of human experience, always observing sexual love from the outside, not from the inside, for fear of the 'risk' involved. Out of that worry came some of his most interesting fiction.

James did not rate 'The Diary' highly enough to include it in the twenty-four volume New York Edition of his *Novels and Tales* (1907-9). Both of the other stories attached to it here were, however, included in Volume XIV of that *magnum opus*, which contained, as he said in its Preface, 'several short fictions of the type I have already found it convenient to refer to as "international" – though I freely recognize, before the array of my productions, of whatever length and whatever brevity, the general applicability of that term.' By 'international' James meant America and Europe. There was, he wrote in the same place, 'no possibility of contrast in the human lot so great as that encountered as we turn back and forth between the distinctively American and the distinctively European outlook.' With the rapid demographic and economic growth of the USA in the nineteenth century, and the development of speedy communications (steamships, railways, tele-graphy) between and within the two continents in the same period, Americans and Europeans were brought into social contact, and conflict, on an unprecedented scale; and James noted that the circumstances of his own life – educated partly in Europe, partly in America, and frequently moving back and forth across the Atlantic in adulthood – had given him 'considerable occasion to appreciate the mixture of manners'. He studied the phenomenon in a variety of ways, and in a variety of social sub-groups. It is not simply a matter of American innocence versus European experience, though that is the basic antithesis. There were cultured American expats who aimed to blend invisibly into the civilised Old World, and were sometimes corrupted by it. There were some *nouveaux-riches* Yankees who exhibited a crude insensitivity to European culture and others who demonstrated superior energy and idealism. The English occupied an ambiguous position between the Americans and Continental Europeans in James' perspective, more sophisticated than the former, less so than the latter, so that in some stories, like 'The Diary', the English characters act out similar roles *vis à vis* 'Europe' to those of American characters in other tales.

It was James' unique mastery of this complex subject that made him appear such an exciting new star on the literary scene in the late 1870s and early 1880s. His first real 'hit' (as he described it himself) was 'Daisy Miller' (1878), a deliciously amusing but finally poignant study of the consequences that could result from the 'mixture of manners', and he quickly followed it up with several other short stories and longer tales playing variations on the international theme – among them 'A Bundle of Letters', first published in the same year as 'The Diary'. This story exploits the comic possibilities of bringing contrasting American and European types together in a single setting – the house of a Parisian family who accommodate paying guests wishing to improve their competence in spoken French – and it will both surprise and delight new readers who think of James as an austerely 'serious' and for-biddingly difficult writer. It is written in the form of letters, a venerable device which goes back to the eighteenth century. As a narrative method it has something in common with the diary, since the letters provide a trace of the correspondents' progress into an unknown future. Narrative, however, is subordinated to character in this story: the reader's pleasure is all in what the characters reveal, often unconsciously, about themselves and each other.

Miss Miranda Hope, a naïve but enterprising young woman from Maine, a proto-feminist, courageous enough to travel to Europe unaccompanied and eager to acquire as much knowledge of the Old World as her limited purse will allow, writes home to her mother. She has come to Paris from England where she thought the position of women was unsatisfactory: those she met had 'a kind of depressed and humiliated tone; a little dull, tame look, as if they were used to being snubbed and bullied, which made me want to give them a good shaking... The men are *remarkably handsome*. (You can show this to William Platt if you like.)' William Platt, we infer from her occasional parentheses ('Tell William Platt I don't care what he does') is a young man with whom she has had some kind of tiff. To Miss Violet Ray, the spoiled New York belle who is staying at the house with her mother, Miranda 'is the most extraordinary specimen of artless Yankeeism that I ever encountered' and she snubs her attempt to be friendly. Louis Leverett is a young American aesthete, evidently a disciple of Pater and Wilde, who is intoxicated with the ambience of Paris. 'The great thing is to *live*, you know...' he assures his friend in Boston. 'There are times... when I feel as if I were really capable of everything – *capable de tout*, as they say here...' His habit of attaching to his English phrases their French equivalents betrays a callow eagerness to cut a cosmopolitan figure, but he draws a vivid picture of the two American girls, 'one of them all elegance, all expensiveness, with an air of high fashion... the other a plain, pure, clear-eyed, straight-waisted, straight-stepping maiden from the heart of New England.' He himself is under the spell of Evelyn Vane, an aristocratic young English woman residing in the house with her brother: 'She is much a woman – *elle est bien femme* as they say here; simpler, softer, rounder, richer than the young girls I spoke of just now.' Miranda admires the melodious voices of Evelyn and her brother, but her feminist, egalitarian opinions seem to them bizarre. Other correspondents include a young Frenchman belonging to the host family who exploits every opportunity to flirt with the unchaperoned American girls, and a German academic who observes the representatives of all the other nations with impartial irony. In the Preface James recalled that this story was written in a couple of days of concentrated work when he was confined to 'the small, shiny, shabby salon of an *hotel garni*' in Paris by a heavy snowstorm. He obviously enjoyed rendering and counterpointing the very different styles and voices of his correspondents, and his glee conveys itself to the reader. 'A Bundle of Letters' was instantly popular with the readers of a magazine called *The Parisian* where it first appeared in December 1879, but unfortunately James was too slow to prevent its being pirated in America. He established his copyright in the following year by publishing it in New York in a small book, paired with 'The Diary of a Man of Fifty', which suggests that he saw the latter as belonging to his 'international' fiction.

Two years later James wrote a companion piece to 'A Bundle of Letters' called 'The Point of View', made up of letters from a number of characters, including some of those in the earlier story, who travel in the opposite direction, from Europe to America. Louis Leverett is rather sadly going home, in the company of Mr Cockerel, a chauvinistic Yankee whose extensive travels have not shaken his conviction that the USA 'is the only country'. On the Atlantic crossing these two young men hover round Aurora Church, a young American who has been brought up in Switzerland and is returning to the homeland with her mother in the hope of acquiring a husband. Other passengers include Mr Antrobus, an English MP and paterfamilias, who is going to study American social and political life, and is befriended by the American Miss Sturdy, self-described as 'single, stout and red in the face' but a shrewd and witty woman. The letters present the contrasting impressions of these travellers, some of them American citizens returning to the country after an interval, some visitors to whom it is all strange and new.

Aurora's mother has been away so long that she almost feels she belongs in the latter category. She is particularly exercised by the freedom enjoyed by young Americans as regards meeting and mixing with the opposite sex, and observes with disapproval a phenomenon, totally alien to the strict supervision of respectable unmarried girls in Europe, which would later mutate into 'dating': 'There is a peculiar custom in this country… it is called "being attentive", and young girls are the object of the attention. It has not necessarily anything to do with projects of marriage.' Aurora for her part is excited by the prospect of being able to go about on her own, and makes a bargain with her mother that she will be allowed to do so as long as the quest for a husband lasts. Miss Sturdy, returning from a long visit to England, has a more nuanced perception of American manners. English girls, she observes, know how to speak but not how to talk; with American girls it is the other way round. Like James himself, she deplores the development of a distinctively American variety of English. 'Of course, a people of fifty millions, who have invented a new civilisation, have a right to a language of their own… But I wish they had made it as pretty as the mother-tongue.'

This story is probably the finest of the three gathered here, full of wit, subtle observation, and insight. It is also very funny: for instance, in dealing with Mr Antrobus' experience of the relaxed arrangements in American sleeping cars, and his insistence on travelling with his own bathtub but without a servant to carry it for him; also in representing the misery of the sensitive Mr Leverett in a huge American hotel where there is an endless supply of that 'unconsoling fluid', iced water, but no civility: 'We are dying of iced water, of hot air, of gas.' One of the delightful surprises of the story is how many of the features of American life James picks out for comment, both complimentary and pejorative, by his correspondents, still strike the visitor today, and he maintains an even-handed balance between the different 'points of view'. In due course that phrase would become a key term in literary criticism of prose fiction, thanks to James' own essays, reviews and prefaces, in which he explained that the effects of fictional events are always determined by the point, or points, of view from which they are perceived. These three stories are exemplary demonstrations of the maxim.

– *David Lodge, 2008*

The Diary of
a Man of Fifty

THE DIARY OF A MAN OF FIFTY

Florence, *April 5th, 1874* – They told me I should find Italy greatly changed; and in seven and twenty years there is room for changes. But to me everything is so perfectly the same that I seem to be living my youth over again; all the forgotten impressions of that enchanting time come back to me. At the moment they were powerful enough; but they afterwards faded away. What in the world became of them? Whatever becomes of such things, in the long intervals of consciousness? Where do they hide themselves away? In what unvisited cupboards and crannies of our being do they preserve themselves? They are like the lines of a letter written in sympathetic ink; hold the letter to the fire for a while and the grateful warmth brings out the invisible words. It is the warmth of this yellow sun of Florence that has been restoring the text of my own young romance; the thing has been lying before me today as a clear, fresh page. There have been moments during the last ten years when I have felt so portentously old, so fagged and finished, that I should have taken as a very bad joke any intimation that this present sense of juvenility was still in store for me. It won't last, at any rate; so I had better make the best of it. But I confess it surprises me. I have led too serious a life; but that perhaps, after all, preserves one's youth. At all events, I have travelled too far, I have worked too hard, I have lived in brutal climates and associated with tiresome people. When a man has reached his fifty-second year without being, materially, the worse for wear – when he has fair health, a fair fortune, a tidy conscience and a complete exemption from embarrassing relatives – I suppose he is bound, in delicacy, to write himself happy. But I confess I shirk this obligation. I have not been miserable; I won't go so far as to say that – or at least as to write it. But happiness – positive happiness – would have been something different. I don't know that it would have been better, by all measurements – that it would have left me better off at the present time. But it certainly would have made this difference – that I should not have been reduced, in pursuit of pleasant images, to disinter a buried episode of more than a quarter of a century ago. I should have found entertainment more – what shall I call it? – more contemporaneous. I should have had a wife and children, and I should not be in the way of making, as the French say, infidelities to the present. Of course it's a great gain to have had an escape, not to have committed an act of thumping folly; and I suppose that, whatever serious step one might have taken at twenty-five, after a struggle, and with a violent effort, and however one's conduct might appear to be justified by events, there would always remain a certain element of regret; a certain sense of loss lurking in the sense of gain; a tendency to wonder, rather wishfully, what *might* have been. What might have been, in this case, would, without doubt, have been very sad, and what has been has been very cheerful and comfortable; but there are nevertheless two or three questions I might ask myself. Why, for instance, have I never married – why have I never been able to care for any woman as I cared for that one? Ah, why are the mountains blue and why is the sunshine warm? Happiness mitigated by impertinent conjectures – that's about my ticket.

6th – I knew it wouldn't last; it's already passing away. But I have spent a delightful day; I have been strolling all over the place. Everything reminds me of something else, and yet of itself at the same time; my imagination makes a great circuit and comes back to the starting point. There is that well-remembered odour of spring in the air, and the flowers, as they used to be, are gathered into great sheaves and stacks, all along the rugged base of the Strozzi Palace. I wandered for an hour in the Boboli Gardens; we went there several times together. I remember all those days individually; they seem to me as yesterday. I found the corner where she always chose to sit – the bench of sun-warmed marble, in front of the screen of ilex, with that exuberant statue of Pomona just beside it. The place is exactly the same, except that poor Pomona has lost one of her tapering fingers. I sat there for half an hour, and it was strange how near to me she seemed. The place was perfectly empty – that is, it was filled with *her*. I closed my eyes and listened; I could almost hear the rustle of her dress on the gravel. Why do we make such an ado about death? What is it, after all, but a sort of refinement of life? She died ten years ago, and yet, as I sat there in the sunny stillness, she was a palpable, audible presence. I went afterwards into the gallery of the palace, and wandered for an hour from room to

4

room. The same great pictures hung in the same places and the same dark frescoes arched above them. Twice, of old, I went there with her; she had a great understanding of art. She understood all sorts of things. Before the Madonna of the Chair I stood a long time. The face is not a particle like hers, and yet it reminded me of her. But everything does that. We stood and looked at it together once for half an hour; I remember perfectly what she said.

8th – Yesterday I felt blue – blue and bored; and when I got up this morning I had half a mind to leave Florence. But I went out into the street, beside the Arno, and looked up and down – looked at the yellow river and the violet hills, and then decided to remain – or rather, I decided nothing. I simply stood gazing at the beauty of Florence, and before I had gazed my fill I was in good humour again, and it was too late to start for Rome. I strolled along the quay, where something presently happened that rewarded me for staying. I stopped in front of a little jeweller's shop, where a great many objects in mosaic were exposed in the window. I stood there for some minutes – I don't know why, for I have no taste for mosaic. In a moment a little girl came and stood beside me – a little girl with a frowsy Italian head, carrying a basket. I turned away, but, as I turned, my eyes happened to fall on her basket. It was covered with a napkin, and on the napkin was pinned a piece of paper, inscribed with an address. This address caught my glance – there was a name on it I knew. It was very legibly written – evidently by a scribe who had made up in zeal what was lacking in skill. *Contessa Salvi-Scarabelli, Via Ghibellina* – so ran the superscription; I looked at it for some moments; it caused me a sudden emotion. Presently the little girl, becoming aware of my attention, glanced up at me, wondering, with a pair of timid brown eyes.

'Are you carrying your basket to the Countess Salvi?' I asked.

The child stared at me. 'To the Countess Scarabelli.'

'Do you know the Countess?'

'Know her?' murmured the child, with an air of small dismay.

'I mean, have you seen her?'

'Yes, I have seen her.' And then, in a moment, with a sudden soft smile – '*E bella!*' said the little girl. She was beautiful herself as she said it.

'Precisely; and is she fair or dark?'

The child kept gazing at me. *'Bionda – bionda,'* she answered, looking about into the golden sunshine for a comparison.

'And is she young?'

'She is not young – like me. But she is not old like – like –'

'Like me, eh? And is she married?'

The little girl began to look wise. 'I have never seen the Signor Conte.'

'And she lives in Via Ghibellina?'

'Sicuro. In a beautiful palace.'

I had one more question to ask, and I pointed it with certain copper coins. 'Tell me a little – is she good?'

The child inspected a moment the contents of her little brown fist. 'It's you who are good,' she answered.

'Ah, but the Countess?' I repeated.

My informant lowered her big brown eyes, with an air of conscientious meditation that was inexpressibly quaint. 'To me she appears so,' she said at last, looking up.

'Ah, then she must be so,' I said, 'because, for your age, you are very intelligent.' And having delivered myself of this compliment I walked away and left the little girl counting her *soldi.*

I walked back to the hotel, wondering how I could learn something about the Contessa Salvi-Scarabelli. In the doorway I found the innkeeper, and near him stood a young man whom I immediately perceived to be a compatriot and with whom, apparently, he had been in conversation.

'I wonder whether you can give me a piece of information,' I said to the landlord. 'Do you know anything about the Count Salvi-Scarabelli?'

The landlord looked down at his boots, then slowly raised his shoulders, with a melancholy smile. 'I have many regrets, dear sir –'

'You don't know the name?'

'I know the name, assuredly. But I don't know the gentleman.'

I saw that my question had attracted the attention of the young Englishman, who looked at me with a good deal of earnestness. He was apparently satisfied with what he saw, for he presently decided to speak.

6

'The Count Scarabelli is dead,' he said, very gravely.

I looked at him a moment; he was a pleasing young fellow. 'And his widow lives,' I observed, 'in Via Ghibellina?'

'I daresay that is the name of the street.' He was a handsome young Englishman, but he was also an awkward one. He wondered who I was and what I wanted, and he did me the honour to perceive that, as regards these points, my appearance was reassuring. But he hesitated, very properly, to talk with a perfect stranger about a lady whom he knew, and he had not the art to conceal his hesitation. I instantly felt it to be singular that though he regarded me as a perfect stranger, I had not the same feeling about him. Whether it was that I had seen him before, or simply that I was struck with his agreeable young face – at any rate, I felt myself, as they say here, in sympathy with him. If I have seen him before I don't remember the occasion, and neither, apparently, does he; I suppose it's only a part of the feeling I have had the last three days about everything. It was this feeling that made me suddenly act as if I had known him a long time.

'Do you know the Countess Salvi?' I asked.

He looked at me a little, and then, without resenting the freedom of my question – 'The Countess Scarabelli, you mean,' he said.

'Yes,' I answered; 'she's the daughter.'

'The daughter is a little girl.'

'She must be grown up now. She must be – let me see – close upon thirty.'

My young Englishman began to smile. 'Of whom are you speaking?'

'I was speaking of the daughter,' I said, understanding his smile. 'But I was thinking of the mother.'

'Of the mother?'

'Of a person I knew twenty-seven years ago – the most charming woman I have ever known. She was the Countess Salvi – she lived in a wonderful old house in Via Ghibellina.'

'A wonderful old house!' my young Englishman repeated.

'She had a little girl,' I went on; 'and the little girl was very fair, like her mother; and the mother and daughter had the same name – Bianca.' I stopped and looked at my companion, and he blushed a little. 'And Bianca Salvi,' I continued, 'was the most charming

7

woman in the world.' He blushed a little more, and I laid my hand on his shoulder. 'Do you know why I tell you this? Because you remind me of what I was when I knew her – when I loved her.' My poor young Englishman gazed at me with a sort of embarrassed and fascinated stare, and still I went on. 'I say that's the reason I told you this – but you'll think it a strange reason. You remind me of my younger self. You needn't resent that – I was a charming young fellow. The Countess Salvi thought so. Her daughter thinks the same of you.'

Instantly, instinctively he raised his hand to my arm. 'Truly?'

'Ah, you are wonderfully like me!' I said, laughing. 'That was just my state of mind. I wanted tremendously to please her.' He dropped his hand and looked away, smiling, but with an air of ingenuous confusion which quickened my interest in him. 'You don't know what to make of me,' I pursued. 'You don't know why a stranger should suddenly address you in this way and pretend to read your thoughts. Doubtless you think me a little cracked. Perhaps I am eccentric; but it's not so bad as that. I have lived about the world a great deal, following my profession, which is that of a soldier. I have been in India, in Africa, in Canada, and I have lived a good deal alone. That inclines people, I think, to sudden bursts of confidence. A week ago I came into Italy, where I spent six months when I was your age. I came straight to Florence – I was eager to see it again, on account of associations. They have been crowding upon me ever so thickly. I have taken the liberty of giving you a hint of them.' The young man inclined himself a little, in silence, as if he had been struck with a sudden respect. He stood and looked away for a moment at the river and the mountains. 'It's very beautiful,' I said.

'Oh, it's enchanting,' he murmured.

'That's the way I used to talk. But that's nothing to you.'

He glanced at me again. 'On the contrary, I like to hear.'

'Well, then, let us take a walk. If you too are staying at this inn, we are fellow-travellers. We will walk down the Arno to the Cascine. There are several things I should like to ask of you.'

My young Englishman assented with an air of almost filial con-fidence, and we strolled for an hour beside the river and through the shady alleys of that lovely wilderness. We had a great deal of talk: it's not only myself, it's my whole situation over again.

'Are you very fond of Italy?' I asked.

He hesitated a moment. 'One can't express that.'

'Just so; I couldn't express it. I used to try – I used to write verses. On the subject of Italy I was very ridiculous.'

'So am I ridiculous,' said my companion.

'No, my dear boy,' I answered, 'we are not ridiculous; we are two very reasonable, superior people.'

'The first time one comes – as I have done – it's a revelation.'

'Oh, I remember well; one never forgets it. It's an introduction to beauty.'

'And it must be a great pleasure,' said my young friend, 'to come back.'

'Yes, fortunately the beauty is always here. What form of it,' I asked, 'do you prefer?'

My companion looked a little mystified; and at last he said, 'I am very fond of the pictures.'

'So was I. And among the pictures, which do you like best?'

'Oh, a great many.'

'So did I; but I had certain favourites.'

Again the young man hesitated a little, and then he confessed that the group of painters he preferred on the whole to all others, was that of the early Florentines.

I was so struck with this that I stopped short. 'That was exactly my taste!' And then I passed my hand into his arm and we went our way again.

We sat down on an old stone bench in the Cascine, and a solemn blank-eyed Hermes, with wrinkles accentuated by the dust of ages, stood above us and listened to our talk.

'The Countess Salvi died ten years ago,' I said.

My companion admitted that he had heard her daughter say so.

'After I knew her she married again,' I added. 'The Count Salvi died before I knew her – a couple of years after their marriage.'

'Yes, I have heard that.'

'And what else have you heard?'

My companion stared at me; he had evidently heard nothing.

'She was a very interesting woman – there are a great many things to be said about her. Later, perhaps, I will tell you. Has the daughter the same charm?'

'You forget,' said my young man, smiling, 'that I have never seen the mother.'

'Very true. I keep confounding. But the daughter – how long have you known her?'

'Only since I have been here. A very short time.'

'A week?'

For a moment he said nothing. 'A month.'

'That's just the answer I should have made. A week, a month – it was all the same to me.'

'I think it is more than a month,' said the young man.

'It's probably six. How did you make her acquaintance?'

'By a letter – an introduction given me by a friend in England.'

'The analogy is complete,' I said. 'But the friend who gave me my letter to Madame de Salvi died many years ago. He, too, admired her greatly. I don't know why it never came into my mind that her daughter might be living in Florence. Somehow I took for granted it was all over. I never thought of the little girl; I never heard what had become of her. I walked past the palace yesterday and saw that it was occupied; but I took for granted it had changed hands.'

'The Countess Scarabelli,' said my friend, 'brought it to her husband as her marriage portion.'

'I hope he appreciated it! There is a fountain in the court, and there is a charming old garden beyond it. The Countess's sitting room looks into that garden. The staircase is of white marble, and there is a medallion by Luca della Robbia set into the wall at the place where it makes a bend. Before you come into the drawing room you stand a moment in a great vaulted place hung round with faded tapestry, paved with bare tiles, and furnished only with three chairs. In the drawing room, above the fireplace, is a superb Andrea del Sarto. The furniture is covered with pale sea-green.'

My companion listened to all this.

'The Andrea del Sarto is there; it's magnificent. But the furniture is in pale red.'

'Ah, they have changed it, then – in twenty-seven years.'

'And there's a portrait of Madame de Salvi,' continued my friend.

I was silent a moment. 'I should like to see that.'

He too was silent. Then he asked, 'Why don't you go and see it? If you knew the mother so well, why don't you call upon the daughter?'

'From what you tell me I am afraid.'

'What have I told you to make you afraid?'

I looked a little at his ingenuous countenance. 'The mother was a very dangerous woman.'

The young Englishman began to blush again. 'The daughter is not,' he said.

'Are you very sure?'

He didn't say he was sure, but he presently inquired in what way the Countess Salvi had been dangerous.

'You must not ask me that,' I answered; 'for, after all, I desire to remember only what was good in her.' And as we walked back I begged him to render me the service of mentioning my name to his friend, and of saying that I had known her mother well and that I asked permission to come and see her.

9th – I have seen that poor boy half a dozen times again, and a most amiable young fellow he is. He continues to represent to me, in the most extraordinary manner, my own young identity; the correspondence is perfect at all points, save that he is a better boy than I. He is evidently acutely interested in his Countess, and leads quite the same life with her that I led with Mme de Salvi. He goes to see her every evening and stays half the night; these Florentines keep the most extraordinary hours. I remember, towards three a.m., Madame de Salvi used to turn me out. 'Come, come,' she would say, 'it's time to go. If you were to stay later people might talk.' I don't know at what time he comes home, but I suppose his evening seems as short as mine did. Today he brought me a message from his Contessa – a very gracious little speech. She remembered often to have heard her mother speak of me – she called me her English friend. All her mother's friends were dear to her, and she begged I would do her the honour to come and see her. She is always at home of an evening. Poor young Stanmer (he is of the

Devonshire Stanmers – a great property) reported this speech verbatim, and of course it can't in the least signify to him that a poor grizzled, battered soldier, old enough to be his father, should come to call upon his *inammorata*. But I remember how it used to matter to me when other men came; that's a point of difference. However, it's only because I'm so old. At twenty-five I shouldn't have been afraid of myself at fifty-two. Camerino was thirty-four – and then the others! She was always at home in the evening, and they all used to come. They were old Florentine names. But she used to let me stay after them all; she thought an old English name as good. What a transcendent coquette!... But *basta così*, as she used to say. I meant to go tonight to Casa Salvi, but I couldn't bring myself to the point. I don't know what I'm afraid of; I used to be in a hurry enough to go there once. I suppose I am afraid of the very look of the place – of the old rooms, the old walls. I shall go tomorrow night. I am afraid of the very echoes.

10th – She has the most extraordinary resemblance to her mother. When I went in I was tremendously startled; I stood staring at her. I have just come home; it is past midnight; I have been all the evening at Casa Salvi. It is very warm – my window is open – I can look out on the river, gliding past in the starlight. So, of old, when I came home, I used to stand and look out. There are the same cypresses on the opposite hills.

Poor young Stanmer was there, and three or four other admirers; they all got up when I came in. I think I had been talked about, and there was some curiosity. But why should I have been talked about? They were all youngish men – none of them of my time. She is a wonderful likeness of her mother; I couldn't get over it. Beautiful like her mother, and yet with the same faults in her face; but with her mother's perfect head and brow and sympathetic, almost pitying eyes. Her face has just that peculiarity of her mother's, which, of all human countenances that I have ever known, was the one that passed most quickly and completely from the expression of gaiety to that of repose. Repose, in her face, always suggested sadness; and while you were watching it with a kind of awe, and wondering of what tragic secret it was the token, it kindled, on the instant, into a radiant Italian smile. The Countess Scarabelli's smiles tonight, however, were almost uninterrupted. She greeted me – divinely, as her mother used to do; and young Stanmer sat in the corner of the sofa – as I used to do – and watched her while she talked. She is thin and very fair, and was dressed in light, vaporous black: that completes the resemblance. The house, the rooms, are almost absolutely the same; there may be changes of detail, but they don't modify the general effect. There are the same precious pictures on the walls of the salon – the same great dusky fresco in the concave ceiling. The daughter is not rich, I suppose, any more than the mother. The furniture is worn and faded, and I was admitted by a solitary servant who carried a twinkling taper before me up the great dark marble staircase.

'I have often heard of you,' said the Countess, as I sat down near her; 'my mother often spoke of you.'

'Often?' I answered. 'I am surprised at that.'

'Why are you surprised? Were you not good friends?'

'Yes, for a certain time – very good friends. But I was sure she had forgotten me.'

'She never forgot,' said the Countess, looking at me intently and smiling. 'She was not like that.'

'She was not like most other women in any way,' I declared.

'Ah, she was charming,' cried the Countess, rattling open her fan. 'I have always been very curious to see you. I have received an impression of you.'

'A good one, I hope.'

She looked at me, laughing, and not answering this: it was just her mother's trick.

'"My Englishman",' she used to call you – "*il mio Inglese*".'

'I hope she spoke of me kindly,' I insisted.

The Countess, still laughing, gave a little shrug, balancing her hand to and fro. 'So-so; I always supposed you had had a quarrel. You don't mind my being frank like this – eh?'

'I delight in it; it reminds me of your mother.'

'Everyone tells me that. But I am not clever like her. You will see for yourself.'

'That speech,' I said, 'completes the resemblance. She was always pretending she was not clever, and in reality –'

'In reality she was an angel, eh? To escape from dangerous comparisons I will admit then that I am clever. That will make a difference. But let us talk of you. You are very – how shall I say it? – very eccentric.'

'Is that what your mother told you?'

'To tell the truth, she spoke of you as a great original. But aren't all Englishmen eccentric? All except that one!' and the Countess pointed to poor Stanmer, in his corner of the sofa.

'Oh, I know just what he is,' I said.

'He's as quiet as a lamb – he's like all the world,' cried the Countess.

'Like all the world – yes. He is in love with you.'

She looked at me with sudden gravity. 'I don't object to your saying that for all the world – but I do for him.'

'Well,' I went on, 'he is peculiar in this: he is rather afraid of you.'

Instantly she began to smile; she turned her face towards Stanmer. He had seen that we were talking about him; he coloured and got up – then came towards us.

'I like men who are afraid of nothing,' said our hostess.

'I know what you want,' I said to Stanmer. 'You want to know what the Signora Contessa says about you.'

Stanmer looked straight into her face, very gravely. 'I don't care a straw what she says.'

'You are almost a match for the Signora Contessa,' I answered. 'She declares she doesn't care a pin's head what you think.'

'I recognise the Countess's style!' Stanmer exclaimed, turning away.

'One would think,' said the Countess, 'that you were trying to make a quarrel between us.'

I watched him move away to another part of the great saloon; he stood in front of the Andrea del Sarto, looking up at it. But he was not seeing it; he was listening to what we might say. I often stood there in just that way. 'He can't quarrel with you, any more than I could have quarrelled with your mother.'

'Ah, but you did. Something painful passed between you.'

'Yes, it was painful, but it was not a quarrel. I went away one day and never saw her again. That was all.'

The Countess looked at me gravely. 'What do you call it when a man does that?'

14

'It depends upon the case.'

'Sometimes,' said the Countess in French, 'it's a *lâcheté*.'

'Yes, and sometimes it's an act of wisdom.'

'And sometimes,' rejoined the Countess, 'it's a mistake.'

I shook my head. 'For me it was no mistake.'

She began to laugh again. 'Caro Signore, you're a great original. What had my poor mother done to you?'

I looked at our young Englishman, who still had his back turned to us and was staring up at the picture. 'I will tell you some other time,' I said.

'I shall certainly remind you; I am very curious to know.' Then she opened and shut her fan two or three times, still looking at me. What eyes they have! 'Tell me a little,' she went on, 'if I may ask without indiscretion. Are you married?'

'No, Signora Contessa.'

'Isn't that at least a mistake?'

'Do I look very unhappy?'

She dropped her head a little to one side. 'For an Englishman – no!'

'Ah,' said I, laughing, 'you are quite as clever as your mother.'

'And they tell me that you are a great soldier,' she continued; 'you have lived in India. It was very kind of you, so far away, to have remembered our poor dear Italy.'

'One always remembers Italy; the distance makes no difference. I remembered it well the day I heard of your mother's death!'

'Ah, that was a sorrow!' said the Countess. 'There's not a day that I don't weep for her. But *che vuole*? She's a saint in paradise.'

'*Sicuro*,' I answered; and I looked some time at the ground. 'But tell me about yourself, dear lady,' I asked at last, raising my eyes. 'You have also had the sorrow of losing your husband.'

'I am a poor widow, as you see. *Che vuole*? My husband died after three years of marriage.'

I waited for her to remark that the late Count Scarabelli was also a saint in paradise, but I waited in vain.

'That was like your distinguished father,' I said.

'Yes, he too died young. I can't be said to have known him. I was but of the age of my own little girl. But I weep for him all the more.'

15

Again I was silent for a moment.

'It was in India too,' I said presently, 'that I heard of your mother's second marriage.'

The Countess raised her eyebrows.

'In India, then, one hears of everything! Did that news please you?'

'Well, since you ask me – no.'

'I understand that,' said the Countess, looking at her open fan. 'I shall not marry again like that.'

'That's what your mother said to me,' I ventured to observe.

She was not offended, but she rose from her seat and stood looking at me a moment. Then –

'You should not have gone away!' she exclaimed.

I stayed for another hour; it is a very pleasant house. Two or three of the men who were sitting there seemed very civil and intelligent; one of them was a major of engineers, who offered me a profusion of information upon the new organisation of the Italian army. While he talked, however, I was observing our hostess, who was talking with the others; very little, I noticed, with her young Inglese. She is altogether charming – full of frankness and freedom, of that inimitable *disinvoltura* which in an Englishwoman would be vulgar, and which in her is simply the perfection of apparent spontaneity. But for all her spontaneity she's as subtle as a needlepoint, and knows tremendously well what she is about. If she is not a consummate coquette… What had she in her head when she said that I should not have gone away? – Poor little Stanmer didn't go away. I left him there at midnight.

12th – I found him today sitting in the church of Santa Croce, into which I wandered to escape from the heat of the sun.

In the nave it was cool and dim; he was staring at the blaze of candles on the great altar, and thinking, I am sure, of his incomparable Countess. I sat down beside him, and after a while, as if to avoid the appearance of eagerness, he asked me how I had enjoyed my visit to Casa Salvi, and what I thought of the *padrona*.

'I think half a dozen things,' I said, 'but I can only tell you one now. She's an enchantress. You shall hear the rest when we have left the church.'

'An enchantress?' repeated Stanmer, looking at me askance.

He is a very simple youth, but who am I to blame him?

'A charmer,' I said; 'a fascinatress!'

He turned away, staring at the altar candles.

'An artist – an actress,' I went on, rather brutally.

He gave me another glance.

'I think you are telling me all,' he said.

'No, no, there is more.' And we sat a long time in silence.

At last he proposed that we should go out; and we passed into the street, where the shadows had begun to stretch themselves.

'I don't know what you mean by her being an actress,' he said, as we turned homeward.

'I suppose not. Neither should I have known, if anyone had said that to me.'

'You are thinking about the mother,' said Stanmer. 'Why are you always bringing *her* in?'

'My dear boy, the analogy is so great; it forces itself upon me.'

He stopped, and stood looking at me with his modest, perplexed young face. I thought he was going to exclaim – 'The analogy be hanged!' – but he said after a moment –

'Well, what does it prove?'

'I can't say it proves anything; but it suggests a great many things.'

'Be so good as to mention a few,' he said, as we walked on.

'You are not sure of her yourself,' I began.

'Never mind that – go on with your analogy.'

'That's a part of it. You *are* very much in love with her.'

'That's a part of it too, I suppose?'

'Yes, as I have told you before. You are in love with her, and yet you can't make her out; that's just where I was with regard to Madame de Salvi.'

'And she too was an enchantress, an actress, an artist, and all the rest of it?'

'She was the most perfect coquette I ever knew, and the most dangerous, because the most finished.'

'What you mean, then, is that her daughter is a finished coquette?'

'I rather think so.'

17

Stanmer walked along for some moments in silence.

'Seeing that you suppose me to be a – a great admirer of the Countess,' he said at last, 'I am rather surprised at the freedom with which you speak of her.'

I confessed that I was surprised at it myself. 'But it's on account of the interest I take in you.'

'I am immensely obliged to you!' said the poor boy.

'Ah, of course you don't like it. That is, you like my interest – I don't see how you can help liking that; but you don't like my freedom. That's natural enough; but, my dear young friend, I want only to help you. If a man had said to me – so many years ago – what I am saying to you, I should certainly also, at first, have thought him a great brute. But after a little, I should have been grateful – I should have felt that he was helping me.'

'You seem to have been very well able to help yourself,' said Stanmer. 'You tell me you made your escape.'

'Yes, but it was at the cost of infinite perplexity – of what I may call keen suffering. I should like to save you all that.'

'I can only repeat – it is really very kind of you.'

'Don't repeat it too often, or I shall begin to think you don't mean it.'

'Well,' said Stanmer, 'I think this, at any rate – that you take an extraordinary responsibility in trying to put a man out of conceit of a woman who, as he believes, may make him very happy.'

I grasped his arm, and we stopped, going on with our talk like a couple of Florentines.

'Do you wish to marry her?'

He looked away, without meeting my eyes. 'It's a great responsibility,' he repeated.

'Before Heaven,' I said, 'I would have married the mother! You are exactly in my situation.'

'Don't you think you rather overdo the analogy?' asked poor Stanmer.

'A little more, a little less – it doesn't matter. I believe you are in my shoes. But of course if you prefer it I will beg a thousand pardons and leave them to carry you where they will.'

He had been looking away, but now he slowly turned his face and met my eyes. 'You have gone too far to retreat; what is it you know about her?'

'About this one – nothing. But about the other –'

'I care nothing about the other!'

'My dear fellow,' I said, 'they are mother and daughter – they are as like as two of Andrea's Madonnas.'

'If they resemble each other, then, you were simply mistaken in the mother.'

I took his arm and we walked on again; there seemed no adequate reply to such a charge. 'Your state of mind brings back my own so completely,' I said presently. 'You admire her – you adore her, and yet, secretly, you mistrust her. You are enchanted with her personal charm, her grace, her wit, her everything; and yet in your private heart you are afraid of her.'

'Afraid of her?'

'Your mistrust keeps rising to the surface; you can't rid yourself of the suspicion that at the bottom of all things she is hard and cruel, and you would be immensely relieved if someone should persuade you that your suspicion is right.'

Stanmer made no direct reply to this; but before we reached the hotel he said – 'What did you ever know about the mother?'

'It's a terrible story,' I answered.

He looked at me askance. 'What did she do?'

'Come to my rooms this evening and I will tell you.'

He declared he would, but he never came. Exactly the way I should have acted!

14th – I went again, last evening, to Casa Salvi, where I found the same little circle, with the addition of a couple of ladies. Stanmer was there, trying hard to talk to one of them, but making, I am sure, a very poor business of it. The Countess – well, the Countess was admirable. She greeted me like a friend of ten years, towards whom familiarity should not have engendered a want of ceremony; she made me sit near her, and she asked me a dozen questions about my health and my occupations.

'I live in the past,' I said. 'I go into the galleries, into the old palaces and the churches. Today I spent an hour in Michael Angelo's chapel at San Lorenzo.'

'Ah yes, that's the past,' said the Countess. 'Those things are very old.'

'Twenty-seven years old,' I answered.

'Twenty-seven? *Altro*!'

'I mean my own past,' I said. 'I went to a great many of those places with your mother.'

'Ah, the pictures are beautiful,' murmured the Countess, glancing at Stanmer.

'Have you lately looked at any of them?' I asked. 'Have you gone to the galleries with *him*?'

She hesitated a moment, smiling. 'It seems to me that your question is a little impertinent. But I think you are like that.'

'A little impertinent? Never. As I say, your mother did me the honour, more than once, to accompany me to the Uffizzi.'

'My mother must have been very kind to you.'

'So it seemed to me at the time.'

'At the time, only?'

'Well, if you prefer, so it seems to me now.'

'Eh,' said the Countess, 'she made sacrifices.'

'To what, cara Signora? She was perfectly free. Your lamented father was dead – and she had not yet contracted her second marriage.'

'If she was intending to marry again, it was all the more reason she should have been careful.'

I looked at her a moment; she met my eyes gravely, over the top of her fan. 'Are *you* very careful?' I said.

She dropped her fan with a certain violence. 'Ah, yes, you are impertinent!'

'Ah no,' I said. 'Remember that I am old enough to be your father; that I knew you when you were three years old. I may surely ask such questions. But you are right; one must do your mother justice. She was certainly thinking of her second marriage.'

'You have not forgiven her that!' said the Countess, very gravely.

'Have you?' I asked, more lightly.

'I don't judge my mother. That is a mortal sin. My stepfather was very kind to me.'

'I remember him,' I said. 'I saw him a great many times – your mother already received him.'

My hostess sat with lowered eyes, saying nothing; but she presently looked up.

'She was very unhappy with my father.'

'That I can easily believe. And your stepfather – is he still living?'

'He died – before my mother.'

'Did he fight any more duels?'

'He was killed in a duel,' said the Countess, discreetly.

It seems almost monstrous, especially as I can give no reason for it – but this announcement, instead of shocking me, caused me to feel a strange exhilaration. Most assuredly, after all these years, I bear the poor man no resentment. Of course I controlled my manner, and simply remarked to the Countess that as his fault had been, so was his punishment. I think, however, that the feeling of which I speak was at the bottom of my saying to her that I hoped that, unlike her mother's, her own brief married life had been happy.

'If it was not,' she said, 'I have forgotten it now.' – I wonder if the late Count Scarabelli was also killed in a duel, and if his adversary… Is it on the books that his adversary, as well, shall perish by the pistol? Which of those gentlemen is he, I wonder? Is it reserved for poor little Stanmer to put a bullet into him? No; poor little Stanmer, I trust, will do as I did. And yet, unfortunately for him, that woman is consummately plausible. She was wonderfully nice last evening; she was really irresistible. Such frankness and freedom, and yet something so soft and womanly; such graceful gaiety, so much of the brightness, without any of the stiffness, of good breeding, and over it all something so picturesquely simple and southern. She is a perfect Italian. But she comes honestly by it. After the talk I have just jotted down she changed her place, and the conversation for half an hour was general. Stanmer indeed said very little; partly, I suppose, because he is shy of talking a foreign tongue. Was I like that – was I so constantly silent? I suspect I was when I was perplexed, and Heaven knows that very often my perplexity was extreme. Before I went away I had a few more words *tête-à-tête* with the Countess.

'I hope you are not leaving Florence yet,' she said; 'you will stay a while longer?'

I answered that I came only for a week, and that my week was over.

'I stay on from day to day, I am so much interested.'

'Eh, it's the beautiful moment. I'm glad our city pleases you!'

'Florence pleases me – and I take a paternal interest in our young friend,' I added, glancing at Stanmer. 'I have become very fond of him.'

'*Bel tipo inglese*,' said my hostess. 'And he is very intelligent; he has a beautiful mind.'

She stood there resting her smile and her clear, expressive eyes upon me.

'I don't like to praise him too much,' I rejoined, 'lest I should appear to praise myself; he reminds me so much of what I was at his age. If your beautiful mother were to come to life for an hour she would see the resemblance.'

She gave me a little amused stare.

'And yet you don't look at all like him!'

'Ah, you didn't know me when I was twenty-five. I was very handsome! And, moreover, it isn't that, it's the mental resemblance. I was ingenuous, candid, trusting, like him.'

'Trusting? I remember my mother once telling me that you were the most suspicious and jealous of men!'

'I fell into a suspicious mood, but I was, fundamentally, not in the least addicted to thinking evil. I couldn't easily imagine any harm of anyone.'

'And so you mean that Mr Stanmer is in a suspicious mood?'

'Well, I mean that his situation is the same as mine.'

The Countess gave me one of her serious looks.

'Come,' she said, 'what was it – this famous situation of yours? I have heard you mention it before.'

'Your mother might have told you, since she occasionally did me the honour to speak of me.'

'All my mother ever told me was that you were a sad puzzle to her.'

At this, of course, I laughed out – I laugh still as I write it.

'Well, then, that was my situation – I was a sad puzzle to a very clever woman.'

'And you mean, therefore, that I am a puzzle to poor Mr Stanmer?'

'He is racking his brains to make you out. Remember it was you who said he was intelligent.'

She looked round at him, and as fortune would have it, his appearance at that moment quite confirmed my assertion. He was lounging back in his chair with an air of indolence rather too marked for a drawing room, and staring at the ceiling with the expression of a man who has just been asked a conundrum. Madame Scarabelli seemed struck with his attitude.

'Don't you see,' I said, 'he can't read the riddle?'

'You yourself,' she answered, 'said he was incapable of thinking evil. I should be sorry to have him think any evil of *me*.'

And she looked straight at me – seriously, appealingly – with her beautiful candid brow.

I inclined myself, smiling, in a manner which might have meant –

'How could that be possible?'

'I have a great esteem for him,' she went on. 'I want him to think well of me. If I am a puzzle to him, do me a little service. Explain me to him.'

'Explain you, dear lady?'

'You are older and wiser than he. Make him understand me.'

She looked deep into my eyes for a moment, and then she turned away.

26th – I have written nothing for a good many days, but meanwhile I have been half a dozen times to Casa Salvi. I have seen a good deal also of my young friend – had a good many walks and talks with him. I have proposed to him to come with me to Venice for a fortnight, but he won't listen to the idea of leaving Florence. He is very happy in spite of his doubts, and I confess that in the perception of his happiness I have lived over again my own. This is so much the case that when, the other day, he at last made up his mind to ask me to tell him the wrong that Madame de Salvi had done me, I rather checked his curiosity. I told him that if he was bent upon knowing I would satisfy him, but that it seemed a pity, just now, to indulge in painful imagery.

'But I thought you wanted so much to put me out of conceit of our friend.'

'I admit I am inconsistent, but there are various reasons for it. In the first place – it's obvious – I am open to the charge of playing a double game. I profess an admiration for the Countess Scarabelli, for I accept her hospitality, and at the same time I attempt to poison your mind; isn't that the proper expression? I can't exactly make up my mind to that, though my admiration for the Countess and my desire to prevent you from taking a foolish step are equally sincere. And then, in the second place you seem to me on the whole so happy! One hesitates to destroy an illusion, no matter how pernicious, that is so delightful while it lasts. These are the rare moments of life. To be young and ardent, in the midst of an Italian spring, and to believe in the moral perfection of a beautiful woman – what an admirable situation! Float with the current; I'll stand on the brink and watch you.'

'Your real reason is that you feel you have no case against the poor lady,' said Stanmer. 'You admire her as much as I do.'

'I just admitted that I admired her. I never said she was a vulgar flirt; her mother was an absolutely scientific one. Heaven knows I admired that! It's a nice point, however, how much one is bound in honour not to warn a young friend against a dangerous woman because one also has relations of civility with the lady.'

'In such a case,' said Stanmer, 'I would break off my relations.'

I looked at him, and I think I laughed.

'Are you jealous of me, by chance?'

He shook his head emphatically.

'Not in the least; I like to see you there, because your conduct contradicts your words.'

'I have always said that the Countess is fascinating.'

'Otherwise,' said Stanmer, 'in the case you speak of I would give the lady notice.'

'Give her notice?'

'Mention to her that you regard her with suspicion, and that you propose to do your best to rescue a simple-minded youth from her wiles. That would be more loyal.' And he began to laugh again.

It is not the first time he has laughed at me, but I have never minded it, because I have always understood it.

'Is that what you recommend me to say to the Countess?' I asked.

'Recommend you!' he exclaimed, laughing again; 'I recommend nothing. I may be the victim to be rescued, but I am at least not a partner to the conspiracy. Besides,' he added in a moment, 'the Countess knows your state of mind.'

'Has she told you so?'

Stanmer hesitated.

'She has begged me to listen to everything you may say against her. She declares that she has a good conscience.'

'Ah,' said I, 'she's an accomplished woman!'

And it is indeed very clever of her to take that tone. Stanmer afterwards assured me explicitly that he has never given her a hint of the liberties I have taken in conversation with – what shall I call it? – with her moral nature; she has guessed them for herself. She must hate me intensely, and yet her manner has always been so charming to me! She is truly an accomplished woman!

May 4th – I have stayed away from Casa Salvi for a week, but I have lingered on in Florence, under a mixture of impulses. I have had it on my conscience not to go near the Countess again – and yet from the moment she is aware of the way I feel about her, it is open war. There need be no scruples on either side. She is as free to use every possible art to entangle poor Stanmer more closely as I am to clip her fine-spun meshes. Under the circumstances, however, we naturally shouldn't meet very cordially. But as regards her meshes, why, after all, should I clip them? It would really be very interesting to see Stanmer swallowed up. I should like to see how he would agree with her after she had devoured him – (to what vulgar imagery, by the way, does curiosity reduce a man!). Let him finish the story in his own way, as I finished it in mine. It is the same story; but why, a quarter of a century later, should it have the same *dénouement*? Let him make his own *dénouement*.

5th – Hang it, however, I don't want the poor boy to be miserable.

6th – Ah, but did my *dénouement* then prove such a happy one?

7th – He came to my room late last night. He was much excited.

'What was it she did to you?' he asked.

I answered him first with another question. 'Have you quarrelled with the Countess?'

But he only repeated his own. 'What was it she did to you?'

'Sit down and I'll tell you.' And he sat there beside the candle, staring at me. 'There was a man always there – Count Camerino.'

'The man she married?'

'The man she married. I was very much in love with her, and yet I didn't trust her. I was sure that she lied; I believed that she could be cruel. Nevertheless, at moments, she had a charm which made it pure pedantry to be conscious of her faults; and while these moments lasted I would have done anything for her. Unfortunately, they didn't last long. But you know what I mean; am I not describing the Scarabelli?'

'The Countess Scarabelli never lied!' cried Stanmer.

'That's just what I would have said to anyone who should have made the insinuation! But I suppose you are not asking me the question you put to me just now from dispassionate curiosity.'

'A man may want to know!' said the innocent fellow.

I couldn't help laughing out. 'This, at any rate, is my story. Camerino was always there; he was a sort of fixture in the house. If I had moments of dislike for the divine Bianca, I had no moments of liking for him. And yet he was a very agreeable fellow, very civil, very intelligent, not in the least disposed to make a quarrel with me. The trouble of course was simply that I was jealous of him. I don't know, however, on what ground I could have quarrelled with him, for I had no definite rights. I can't say what I expected – I can't say what, as the matter stood, I was prepared to do. With my name and my prospects, I might perfectly have offered her my hand. I am not sure that she would have accepted it – I am by no means clear that she wanted that. But she wanted, wanted keenly, to attach me to her; she wanted to have me about. I should have been capable of giving up everything – England, my career, my family – simply to devote myself to her, to live near her and see her every day.'

'Why didn't you do it, then?' asked Stanmer.

'Why don't you?'

'To be a proper rejoinder to my question,' he said, rather neatly, 'yours should be asked twenty-five years hence.'

'It remains perfectly true that at a given moment I was capable of doing as I say. That was what she wanted – a rich, susceptible, credulous, convenient young Englishman established near her *en permanence*. And yet,' I added, 'I must do her complete justice. I honestly believe she was fond of me.' At this Stanmer got up and walked to the window; he stood looking out a moment, and then he turned round. 'You know she was older than I,' I went on. 'Madame Scarabelli is older than you. One day in the garden, her mother asked me in an angry tone why I disliked Camerino; for I had been at no pains to conceal my feeling about him, and something had just happened to bring it out. "I dislike him," I said, "because you like him so much." "I assure you I don't like him," she answered. "He has all the appearance of being your lover," I retorted. It was a brutal speech, certainly, but any other man in my place would have made it. She took it very strangely; she turned pale, but she was not indignant. "How can he be my lover after what he has done?" she asked. "What has he done?" She hesitated a good while, then she said: "He killed my husband." "Good heavens!" I cried. "And you receive him!" Do you know what she said? She said, "*Che vuole?*"'

'Is that all?' asked Stanmer.

'No; she went on to say that Camerino had killed Count Salvi in a duel, and she admitted that her husband's jealousy had been the occasion of it. The Count, it appeared, was a monster of jealousy – he had led her a dreadful life. He himself, meanwhile, had been anything but irreproachable; he had done a mortal injury to a man of whom he pretended to be a friend, and this affair had become notorious. The gentleman in question had demanded satisfaction for his outraged honour; but for some reason or other (the Countess, to do her justice, did not tell me that her husband was a coward), he had not as yet obtained it. The duel with Camerino had come on first; in an access of jealous fury the Count had struck Camerino in the face; and this outrage, I know not how justly, was deemed expiable before the other. By an extraordinary arrangement (the Italians have certainly no sense of fair play) the other man was allowed to be Camerino's second. The duel was fought with swords, and the Count received a wound of which, though at first it was not expected to be fatal, he died on the following day. The matter was hushed up as much as possible for the sake of the Countess's good name, and so successfully that it was presently observed that, among the public, the other gentleman had the credit of having put his blade through M. de Salvi. This gentleman took a fancy not to contradict the impression, and it was allowed to subsist. So long as *he* consented, it was of course in Camerino's interest not to contradict it, as it left him much more free to keep up his intimacy with the Countess.'

Stanmer had listened to all this with extreme attention. 'Why didn't *she* contradict it?'

I shrugged my shoulders. 'I am bound to believe it was for the same reason. I was horrified, at any rate, by the whole story. I was extremely shocked at the Countess's want of dignity in continuing to see the man by whose hand her husband had fallen.'

'The husband had been a great brute, and it was not known,' said Stanmer.

'Its not being known made no difference. And as for Salvi having been a brute, that is but a way of saying that his wife, and the man whom his wife subsequently married, didn't like him.'

Stanmer looked extremely meditative; his eyes were fixed on mine. 'Yes, that marriage is hard to get over. It was not becoming.'

'Ah,' said I, 'what a long breath I drew when I heard of it! I remember the place and the hour. It was at a hill station in India, seven years after I had left Florence. The post brought me some English papers, and in one of them was a letter from Italy, with a lot of so-called "fashionable intelligence". There, among various scandals in high life, and other delectable items, I read that the Countess Bianca Salvi, famous for some years as the presiding genius of the most agreeable *salon* in Florence, was about to bestow her hand upon Count Camerino, a distinguished Bolognese. Ah, my dear boy, it was a tremendous escape! I had been ready to marry the woman who was capable of that! But my instinct had warned me, and I had trusted my instinct.'

'"Instinct's everything," as Falstaff says!' And Stanmer began to laugh. 'Did you tell Madame de Salvi that your instinct was against her?'

'No; I told her that she frightened me, shocked me, horrified me.'

'That's about the same thing. And what did she say?'

'She asked me what I would have? I called her friendship with Camerino a scandal, and she answered that her husband had been a brute. Besides, no one knew it; therefore it was no scandal. Just *your* argument! I retorted that this was odious reasoning, and that she had no moral sense. We had a passionate argument, and I declared I would never see her again. In the heat of my displeasure I left Florence, and I kept my vow. I never saw her again.'

'You couldn't have been much in love with her,' said Stanmer.

'I was not – three months after.'

'If you had been you would have come back – three days after.'

'So doubtless it seems to you. All I can say is that it was the great effort of my life. Being a military man, I have had on various occasions to face the enemy. But it was not then I needed my resolution; it was when I left Florence in a post-chaise.'

Stanmer turned about the room two or three times, and then he said: 'I don't understand! I don't understand why she should have told you that Camerino had killed her husband. It could only damage her.'

'She was afraid it would damage her more that I should think he was her lover. She wished to say the thing that would most effectually persuade me that he was not her lover – that he could never be. And then she wished to get the credit of being very frank.'

'Good heavens, how you must have analysed her!' cried my companion, staring.

'There is nothing so analytic as disillusionment. But there it is. She married Camerino.'

'Yes, I don't like that,' said Stanmer. He was silent a while, and then he added – 'Perhaps she wouldn't have done so if you had remained.'

He has a little innocent way! 'Very likely she would have dispensed with the ceremony,' I answered, dryly.

'Upon my word,' he said, 'you *have* analysed her!'

'You ought to be grateful to me. I have done for you what you seem unable to do for yourself.'

'I don't see any Camerino in my case,' he said.

'Perhaps among those gentlemen I can find one for you.'

'Thank you,' he cried. 'I'll take care of that myself!' And he went away – satisfied, I hope.

10th – He's an obstinate little wretch; it irritates me to see him sticking to it. Perhaps he is looking for his Camerino. I shall leave him, at any rate, to his fate; it is growing insupportably hot.

11th – I went this evening to bid farewell to the Scarabelli. There was no one there; she was alone in her great dusky drawing room, which was lighted only by a couple of candles, with the immense windows open over the garden. She was dressed in white; she was deucedly pretty. She asked me, of course, why I had been so long without coming.

'I think you say that only for form,' I answered. 'I imagine you know.'

'*Chè*! What have I done?'

'Nothing at all. You are too wise for that.'

She looked at me a while. 'I think you are a little crazy.'

'Ah no, I am only too sane. I have too much reason rather than too little.'

'You have, at any rate, what we call a fixed idea.'

'There is no harm in that so long as it's a good one.'

'But yours is abominable!' she exclaimed, with a laugh.

'Of course you can't like me or my ideas. All things considered, you have treated me with wonderful kindness, and I thank you and kiss your hands. I leave Florence tomorrow.'

'I won't say I'm sorry!' she said, laughing again. 'But I am very glad to have seen you. I always wondered about you. You are a curiosity.'

'Yes, you must find me so. A man who can resist your charms! The fact is, I can't. This evening you are enchanting; and it is the first time I have been alone with you.'

She gave no heed to this; she turned away. But in a moment she came back, and stood looking at me, and her beautiful solemn eyes seemed to shine in the dimness of the room.

'How *could* you treat my mother so?' she asked.

'Treat her so?'

'How could you desert the most charming woman in the world?'

'It was not a case of desertion; and if it had been it seems to me she was consoled.'

At this moment there was the sound of a step in the antechamber, and I saw that the Countess perceived it to be Stanmer's.

'That wouldn't have happened,' she murmured. 'My poor mother needed a protector.'

Stanmer came in, interrupting our talk, and looking at me, I thought, with a little air of bravado. He must think me indeed a tiresome, meddlesome bore; and upon my word, turning it all over, I wonder at his docility. After all, he's five-and-twenty – and yet I *must* add, it *does* irritate me – the way he sticks! He was followed in a moment by two or three of the regular Italians, and I made my visit short.

'Goodbye, Countess,' I said, and she gave me her hand in silence. 'Do *you* need a protector?' I added, softly.

She looked at me from head to foot, and then, almost angrily –

'Yes, Signore.'

But, to deprecate her anger, I kept her hand an instant, and then bent my venerable head and kissed it. I think I appeased her.

BOLOGNA, *14th* – I left Florence on the 11th, and have been here these three days. Delightful old Italian town – but it lacks the charm of my Florentine secret.

I wrote that last entry five days ago, late at night, after coming back from Casa Salvi. I afterwards fell asleep in my chair; the night was half over when I woke up. Instead of going to bed, I stood a long time at the window, looking out at the river. It was a warm, still night, and the first faint streaks of sunrise were in the sky. Presently I heard a slow footstep beneath my window, and looking down, made out by the aid of a street lamp that Stanmer was but just coming home. I called to him to come to my rooms, and, after an interval, he made his appearance.

'I want to bid you goodbye,' I said. 'I shall depart in the morning. Don't go to the trouble of saying you are sorry. Of course you are not. I must have bullied you immensely.'

He made no attempt to say he was sorry, but he said he was very glad to have made my acquaintance.

'Your conversation,' he said, with his little innocent air, 'has been very suggestive.'

'Have you found Camerino?' I asked, smiling.

'I have given up the search.'

'Well,' I said, 'some day when you find that you have made a great mistake, remember I told you so.'

He looked for a minute as if he were trying to anticipate that day by the exercise of his reason.

'Has it ever occurred to you that *you* may have made a great mistake?'

'Oh yes; everything occurs to one sooner or later.'

That's what I said to him; but I didn't say that the question, pointed by his candid young countenance, had, for the moment, a greater force than it had ever had before.

And then he asked me whether, as things had turned out, I myself had been so especially happy.

PARIS, *December 17th* – A note from young Stanmer, whom I saw in Florence – a remarkable little note, dated Rome, and worth transcribing.

> *My dear General, – I have it at heart to tell you that I was married a week ago to the Countess Salvi-Scarabelli. You talked me into a great muddle; but a month after that it was all very clear. Things that involve a risk are like the Christian faith; they must be seen from the inside. Yours ever, E. S.*
>
> *P.S. – A fig for analogies unless you can find an analogy for my happiness!*

His happiness makes him very clever. I hope it will last – I mean his cleverness, not his happiness.

LONDON, *April 19th, 1877* – Last night, at Lady H—'s, I met Edmund Stanmer, who married Bianca Salvi's daughter. I heard the other day that they had come to England. A handsome young fellow, with a fresh contented face. He reminded me of Florence, which I didn't pretend to forget; but it was rather awkward, for I remember I used to disparage that woman to him. I had a complete theory about her. But he didn't seem at all stiff; on the contrary, he appeared to enjoy our encounter. I asked him if his wife were there. I had to do that.

'Oh yes, she's in one of the other rooms. Come and make her acquaintance; I want you to know her.'

'You forget that I do know her.'

'Oh no, you don't; you never did.' And he gave a little significant laugh.

I didn't feel like facing the *ci-devant* Scarabelli at that moment; so I said that I was leaving the house, but that I would do myself the honour of calling upon his wife. We talked for a minute of something else, and then, suddenly breaking off and looking at me, he laid his hand on my arm. I must do him the justice to say that he looked felicitous.

'Depend upon it, you were wrong!' he said.

'My dear young friend,' I answered, 'imagine the alacrity with which I concede it.'

Something else again was spoken of, but in an instant he repeated his movement.

'Depend upon it you were wrong.'

'I am sure the Countess has forgiven me,' I said, 'and in that case you ought to bear no grudge. As I have had the honour to say, I will call upon her immediately.'

'I was not alluding to my wife,' he answered. 'I was thinking of your own story.'

'My own story?'

'So many years ago. Was it not rather a mistake?'

I looked at him a moment; he's positively rosy.

'That's not a question to solve in a London crush.'

And I turned away.

22nd – I haven't yet called on the *ci-devant*; I am afraid of finding her at home. And that boy's words have been thrumming in my ears – 'Depend upon it, you were wrong. Wasn't it rather a mistake?' *Was* I wrong – *was* it a mistake? Was I too cautions – too suspicious – too logical? Was it really a protector she needed – a man who might have helped her? Would it have been for his benefit to believe in her, and was her fault only that I had forsaken her? Was the poor woman very unhappy? God forgive me, how the questions come crowding in! If I marred her happiness, I certainly didn't make my own. And I might have made it – eh? That's a charming discovery for a man of my age!

A BUNDLE OF LETTERS

I
From MISS MIRANDA HOPE, *in Paris,*
to MRS ABRAHAM C. HOPE, *at Bangor, Maine.*
September 5th, 1879

MY DEAR MOTHER –

I have kept you posted as far as Tuesday week last, and, although my letter will not have reached you yet, I will begin another before my news accumulates too much. I am glad you show my letters round in the family, for I like them all to know what I am doing, and I can't write to everyone, though I try to answer all reasonable expectations. But there are a great many unreasonable ones, as I suppose you know – not yours, dear mother, for I am bound to say that you never required of me more than was natural. You see you are reaping your reward: I write to you before I write to anyone else.

There is one thing, I hope – that you don't show any of my letters to William Platt. If he wants to see any of my letters, he knows the right way to go to work. I wouldn't have him see one of these letters, written for circulation in the family, for anything in the world. If he wants one for himself, he has got to write to me first. Let him write to me first, and then I will see about answering him. You can show him this if you like; but if you show him anything more, I will never write to you again.

I told you in my last about my farewell to England, my crossing the channel, and my first impressions of Paris. I have thought a great deal about that lovely England since I left it, and all the famous historic scenes I visited; but I have come to the conclusion that it is not a country in which I should care to reside. The position of woman does not seem to me at all satisfactory, and that is a point, you know, on which I feel very strongly. It seems to me that in England they play a very faded-out part, and those with whom I conversed had a kind of depressed and humiliated tone; a little dull, tame look, as if they were used to being snubbed and bullied, which made me want to give them a good shaking. There are a great many people – and a great many things, too – over here that I should like to perform that operation upon. I should like to shake the starch out of some of them, and the dust out of the others. I know fifty girls in Bangor that come much more up to my notion of the stand a truly noble woman should take, than those young ladies in England. But they had a most lovely way of speaking (in England), and the men are *remarkably handsome*. (You can show this to William Platt, if you like.)

I gave you my first impressions of Paris, which quite came up to my expectations, much as I had heard and read about it. The objects of interest are extremely numerous, and the climate is remarkably cheerful and sunny. I should say the position of woman here was considerably higher, though by no means coming up to the American standard. The manners of the people are in some respects extremely peculiar, and I feel at last that I am indeed in *foreign parts*. It is, however, a truly elegant city (very superior to New York), and I have spent a great deal of time in visiting the various monuments and palaces. I won't give you an account of all my wanderings, though I have been most indefatigable; for I am keeping, as I told you before, a most *exhaustive* journal, which I will allow you the *privilege* of reading on my return to Bangor. I am getting on remarkably well, and I must say I am sometimes surprised at my universal good fortune. It only shows what a little energy and common sense will accomplish. I have discovered none of these objections to a young lady travelling in Europe by herself, of which we heard so much before I left, and I don't expect I ever shall, for I certainly don't mean to look for them. I know what I want, and I always manage to get it.

I have received a great deal of politeness – some of it really most pressing, and I have experienced no drawbacks whatever. I have made a great many pleasant acquaintances in travelling round (both ladies and gentlemen), and had a great many most interesting talks. I have collected a great deal of information, for which I refer you to my journal. I assure you my journal is going to be a splendid thing. I do just exactly as I do in Bangor, and I find I do perfectly right; and at any rate, I don't care if I don't. I didn't come to Europe to lead a merely conventional life; I could do that at Bangor. You know I never *would* do it at Bangor, so it isn't likely I am going to make myself miserable over here. So long as I accomplish what I desire, and make my money hold out, I shall regard the thing as a success. Sometimes I feel rather lonely, especially in the evening; but I generally manage to interest myself in something or in someone. In the evening I usually read up about the objects of interest I have visited during the day, or I post up my journal. Sometimes I go to the theatre; or else I play the piano in the public parlour. The public parlour at the hotel isn't much; but the piano is better than that fearful old thing at the Sebago House. Sometimes I go downstairs and talk to the lady who keeps the books – a French lady, who is remarkably polite. She is very pretty, and always wears a black dress, with the most beautiful fit; she speaks a little English; she tells me she had to learn it in order to converse with the Americans who come in such numbers to this hotel. She has given me a great deal of information about the position of woman in France, and much of it is very encouraging. But she has told me at the same time some things that I should not like to write to you (I am hesitating even about putting them into my journal), especially if my letters are to be handed round in the family. I assure you they appear to talk about things here that we never think of mentioning at Bangor, or even of thinking about. She seems to think she can tell me everything, because I told her I was travelling for general culture. Well, I *do* want to know so much that it seems sometimes as if I wanted to know everything; and yet there are some things that I think I don't want to know. But, as a general thing, everything is intensely interesting; I don't mean only everything that this French lady tells me, but everything I see and hear for myself. I feel really as if I should gain all I desire.

I meet a great many Americans, who, as a general thing, I must say, are not as polite to me as the people over here. The people over here – especially the gentlemen – are much more what I should call *attentive*. I don't know whether Americans are more *sincere*; I haven't yet made up my mind about that. The only drawback I experience is when Americans sometimes express surprise that I should be travelling round alone; so you see it doesn't come from Europeans. I always have my answer ready: 'For general culture, to acquire the languages, and to see Europe for myself'; and that generally seems to satisfy them. Dear mother, my money holds out very well, and it *is* real interesting.

II

From the same to the same
September 16th

Since I last wrote to you I have left that hotel, and come to live in a French family. It's a kind of boarding house combined with a kind of school; only it's not like an American boarding house, nor like an American school either. There are four or five people here that have come to learn the language – not to take lessons, but to have an opportunity for conversation. I was very glad to come to such a place, for I had begun to realise that I was not making much progress with the French. It seemed to me that I should feel ashamed to have spent two months in Paris, and not to have acquired more insight into the language. I had always heard so much of French conversation, and I found I was having no more opportunity to practise it than if I had remained at Bangor. In fact, I used to hear a great deal more at Bangor, from those French Canadians that came down to cut the ice, than I saw I should ever hear at that hotel. The lady that kept the books seemed to want so much to talk to me in English (for the sake of practice, too, I suppose), that I couldn't bear to let her know I didn't like it. The chambermaid was Irish, and all the waiters were German, so that I never heard a word of French spoken. I suppose you might hear a great deal in the shops; only, as I don't buy anything – I prefer to spend my money for purposes of culture – I don't have that advantage.

I have been thinking some of taking a teacher, but I am well acquainted with the grammar already, and teachers always keep you bothering over the verbs. I was a good deal troubled, for I felt as if I didn't want to go away without having, at least, got a general idea of French conversation. The theatre gives you a good deal of insight, and, as I told you in my last, I go a good deal to places of amusement. I find no difficulty whatever in going to such places alone, and am always treated with the politeness which, as I told you before, I encounter everywhere. I see plenty of other ladies alone (mostly French), and they generally seem to be enjoying themselves as much as I. But, at the theatre, everyone talks so fast that I can scarcely make out what they say; and, besides, there are a great many vulgar expressions which it is unnecessary to learn. But it was the theatre, nevertheless, that put me on the track. The very next day after I wrote to you last, I went to the Palais Royal, which is one of the principal theatres in Paris. It is very small, but it is very celebrated, and in my guidebook it is marked with *two stars*, which is a sign of importance attached only to *first-class* objects of interest. But after I had been there half an hour I found I couldn't understand a single word of the play, they gabbled it off so fast, and they made use of such peculiar expressions. I felt a good deal disappointed and troubled – I was afraid I shouldn't gain all I had come for. But while I was thinking it over – thinking what I *should* do – I heard two gentlemen talking behind me. It was between the acts, and I couldn't help listening to what they said. They were talking English, but I guess they were Americans.

'Well,' said one of them, 'it all depends on what you are after. I'm after French. That's what I'm after.'

'Well,' said the other, 'I'm after Art.'

'Well,' said the first, 'I'm after Art too; but I'm after French most.'

Then, dear mother, I am sorry to say the second one swore a little. He said, 'Oh, damn French!'

'No, I won't damn French,' said his friend. 'I'll acquire it – that's what I'll do with it. I'll go right into a family.'

'What family'll you go into?'

'Into some French family. That's the only way to do – to go to some place where you can talk. If you're after Art, you want to stick to the galleries; you want to go right through the Louvre, room by room; you want to take a room a day, or something of that sort. But, if you want to acquire French, the thing is to look out for a family. There are lots of French families here that take you to board and teach you. My second cousin – that young lady I told you about – she got in with a crowd like that, and they booked her right up in three months. They just took her right in and they talked to her. That's what they do to you; they set you right down and they talk *at* you. You've got to understand them; you can't help yourself. That family my cousin was with has moved away somewhere, or I should try and get in with them. They were very smart people, that family; after she left, my cousin corresponded with them in French. But I mean to find some other crowd, if it takes a lot of trouble!'

I listened to all this with great interest, and when he spoke about his cousin I was on the point of turning around to ask him the address of the family that she was with; but the next moment he said they had moved away, so I sat still. The other gentleman, however, didn't seem to be affected in the same way as I was.

'Well,' he said, 'you may follow up that if you like. I mean to follow up the pictures. I don't believe there is ever going to be any considerable demand in the United States for French; but I can promise you that in about ten years there'll be a big demand for Art! And it won't be temporary either.'

That remark may be very true, but I don't care anything about the demand. I want to know French for its own sake. I don't want to think I have been all this while without having gained an insight... The very next day, I asked the lady who kept the books at the hotel whether she knew of any family that could take me to board and give me the benefit of their conversation. She instantly threw up her hands, with several little shrill cries (in their French way, you know), and told me that her dearest friend kept a regular place of that kind. If she had known I was looking out for such a place she would have told me before; she had not spoken of it herself, because she didn't wish to injure the hotel by being the cause of my going away. She told me this was a charming family, who had often received American ladies (and others as well) who wished to follow up the language, and she was sure I should be delighted with them. So she gave me their address, and offered to go with me to introduce me. But I was in such a hurry that I went off by myself, and I had no trouble in finding these good people. They were delighted to receive me, and I was very much pleased with what I saw of them. They seemed to have plenty of conversation, and there will be no trouble about that.

I came here to stay about three days ago, and by this time I have seen a great deal of them. The price of board struck me as rather high; but I must remember that a quantity of conversation is thrown in. I have a very pretty little room – without any carpet, but with seven mirrors, two clocks, and five curtains. I was rather disappointed after I arrived to find that there are several other Americans here for the same purpose as myself. At least there are three Americans and two English people;

and also a German gentleman. I am afraid, therefore, our conversation will be rather mixed, but I have not yet time to judge. I try to talk with Madame de Maisonrouge all I can (she is the lady of the house, and the *real* family consists only of herself and her two daughters). They are all most elegant, interesting women, and I am sure we shall become intimate friends. I will write you more about them in my next. Tell William Platt I don't care what he does.

III
From MISS VIOLET RAY, *in Paris,*
to MISS AGNES RICH, *in New York*
September 21st

We had hardly got here when father received a telegram saying he would have to come right back to New York. It was for something about his business – I don't know exactly what; you know I never understand those things, never want to. We had just got settled at the hotel, in some charming rooms, and mother and I, as you may imagine, were greatly annoyed. Father is extremely fussy, as you know, and his first idea, as soon as he found he should have to go back, was that we should go back with him. He declared he would never leave us in Paris alone, and that we must return and come out again. I don't know what he thought would happen to us; I suppose he thought we should be too extravagant. It's father's theory that we are always running up bills, whereas a little observation would show him that we wear the same old *rags* FOR MONTHS. But father has no observation; he has nothing but theories. Mother and I, however, have, fortunately, a great deal of *practice*, and we succeeded in making him understand that we wouldn't budge from Paris, and that we would rather be chopped into small pieces than cross that dreadful ocean again. So, at last, he decided to go back alone, and to leave us here for three months. But, to show you how fussy he is, he refused to let us stay at the hotel, and insisted that we should go into a *family*. I don't know what put such an idea into his head, unless it was some advertisement that he saw in one of the American papers that are published here.

There are families here who receive American and English people to live with them, under the pretence of teaching them French. You may imagine what people they are – I mean the families themselves. But the Americans who choose this peculiar manner of seeing Paris must be actually just as bad. Mother and I were horrified, and declared that *main force* should not remove us from the hotel. But Father has a way of arriving at his ends which is more efficient than violence. He worries and fusses; he 'nags', as we used to say at school; and, when Mother and I are quite worn out, his triumph is assured. Mother is usually worn out more easily than I, and she ends by siding with father; so that, at last, when they combine their forces against poor little me, I have to succumb. You should have heard the way Father went on about this 'family' plan; he talked to everyone he saw about it; he used to go round to the banker's and talk to the people there – the people in the post office; he used to try and exchange ideas about it with the waiters at the hotel. He said it would be more safe, more respectable, more economical; that I should perfect my French; that Mother would learn how a French household is conducted; that he should feel more easy, and five hundred reasons more. They were none of them good, but that made no difference. It's all humbug, his talking about economy, when everyone knows that business in America has completely recovered, that the prostration is all over, and that *immense fortunes* are being made. We have been economising for the last five years, and I supposed we came abroad to reap the benefits of it.

As for my French, it is quite as perfect as I want it to be. (I assure you I am often surprised at my own fluency, and, when I get a little more practice in the genders and the idioms, I shall do very well in this respect.) To make a long story short, however, father carried his point, as usual; mother basely deserted me at the last moment, and, after holding out alone for three days, I told them to do with me what they pleased! Father lost three steamers in succession by remaining in Paris to argue with me. You know he is like the schoolmaster in Goldsmith's 'Deserted Village' – 'e'en though vanquished, he would argue still'. He and Mother went to look at some seventeen families (they had got the addresses somewhere), while I retired to my sofa, and would have nothing to do with it. At last they made arrangements, and

I was transported to the establishment from which I now write you. I write you from the bosom of a Parisian ménage – from the depths of a second-rate boarding house.

Father only left Paris after he had seen us what he calls comfortably settled here, and had informed Madame de Maisonrouge (the mistress of the establishment – the head of the 'family') that he wished my French pronunciation especially attended to. The pronunciation, as it happens, is just what I am most at home in; if he had said my genders or my idioms there would have been some sense. But poor father has no tact, and this defect is especially marked since he has been in Europe. He will be absent, however, for three months, and mother and I shall breathe more freely; the situation will be less intense. I must confess that we breathe more freely than I expected, in this place, where we have been for about a week. I was sure, before we came, that it would prove to be an establishment of the *lowest description*; but I must say that, in this respect, I am agreeably disappointed. The French are so clever that they know even how to manage a place of this kind. Of course it is very disagreeable to live with strangers, but as, after all, if I were not staying with Madame de Maisonrouge I should not be living in the Faubourg St Germain, I don't know that from the point of view of exclusiveness it is any great loss to be here.

Our rooms are very prettily arranged, and the table is remarkably good. Mamma thinks the whole thing – the place and the people, the manners and customs – very amusing; but mamma is very easily amused. As for me, you know, all that I ask is to be let alone, and not to have people's society *forced upon me*. I have never wanted for society of my own choosing, and, so long as I retain possession of my faculties, I don't suppose I ever shall. As I said, however, the place is very well managed, and I succeed in doing as I please, which, you know, is my most cherished pursuit. Madame de Maisonrouge has a great deal of tact – much more than poor father. She is what they call here a *belle femme*, which means that she is a tall, ugly woman, with style. She dresses very well, and has a great deal of talk; but, though she is a very good imitation of a lady, I never see her behind the dinner table, in the evening, smiling and bowing, as the people come in, and looking all the while at the dishes and the servants, without thinking of a *dame de comptoir* blooming in a corner of a shop or a restaurant. I am sure that, in spite of her fine name, she was once a *dame de comptoir*. I am also sure that, in spite of her smiles and the pretty things she says to everyone, she hates us all, and would like to murder us. She is a hard, clever Frenchwoman, who would like to amuse herself and enjoy her Paris, and she must be bored to death at passing all her time in the midst of stupid English people who mumble broken French at her. Some day she will poison the soup or the *vin rouge*, but I hope that will not be until after Mother and I shall have left her. She has two daughters, who, except that one is decidedly pretty, are meagre imitations of herself.

The 'family', for the rest, consists altogether of our beloved compatriots, and of still more beloved Englanders. There is an Englishman here, with his sister, and they seem to be rather nice people. He is remarkably handsome, but excessively affected and patronising, especially to us Americans; and I hope to have a chance of biting his head off before long. The sister is very pretty, and, apparently, very nice; but, in costume, she is Britannia incarnate. There is a very pleasant little Frenchman – when they are nice they are charming – and a German doctor, a big, blond man, who looks like a great white bull; and two Americans, besides mother and me. One of them is a young man from Boston – an aesthetic young man, who talks about its being 'a real Corot day', etc., and a young woman – a girl, a female, I don't know what to call her – from Vermont, or Minnesota, or some such place. This young woman is the most extraordinary specimen of artless Yankeeism that I ever encountered; she is really too horrible. I have been three times to Clémentine about your underskirt, etc.

IV
From LOUIS LEVERETT, *in Paris,*
to HARVARD TREMONT, *in Boston*
September 25th

MY DEAR HARVARD –
I have carried out my plan, of which I gave you a hint in my last, and I only regret that I should not have done it before. It is human nature,

after all, that is the most interesting thing in the world, and it only reveals itself to the truly earnest seeker. There is a want of earnestness in that life of hotels and railroad trains, which so many of our countrymen are content to lead in this strange Old World, and I was distressed to find how far I, myself, had been led along the dusty, beaten track. I had, however, constantly wanted to turn aside into more unfrequented ways; to plunge beneath the surface and see what I should discover. But the opportunity had always been missing; somehow, I never meet those opportunities that we hear about and read about – the things that happen to people in novels and biographies. And yet I am always on the watch to take advantage of any opening that may present itself; I am always looking out for experiences, for sensations – I might almost say for adventures.

The great thing is to *live*, you know – to feel, to be conscious of one's possibilities, not to pass through life mechanically and insensibly, like a letter through the post office. There are times, my dear Harvard, when I feel as if I were really capable of everything – *capable de tout*, as they say here – of the greatest excesses as well as the greatest heroism. Oh, to be able to say that one has lived – *qu'on a vécu*, as they say here – that idea exercises an indefinable attraction for me. You will, perhaps, reply, it is easy to say it; but the thing is to make people believe you! And, then, I don't want any second-hand, spurious sensations. I want the knowledge that leaves a trace – that leaves strange scars and stains and reveries behind it! But I am afraid I shock you, perhaps even frighten you.

If you repeat my remarks to any of the West Cedar Street circle, be sure you tone them down as your discretion will suggest. For yourself, you will know that I have always had an intense desire to see something of *real French life*. You are acquainted with my great sympathy with the French; with my natural tendency to enter into the French way of looking at life. I sympathise with the artistic temperament; I remember you used sometimes to hint to me that you thought my own temperament too artistic. I don't think that in Boston there is any real sympathy with the artistic temperament; we tend to make everything a matter of right and wrong. And in Boston one can't *live* – *on ne peut pas vivre*, as they say here. I don't mean one can't reside – for a great many people manage that; but one can't live aesthetically – I may almost venture to say, sensuously. This is why I have always been so much drawn to the French, who are so aesthetic, so sensuous. I am so sorry that Théophile Gautier has passed away. I should have liked so much to go and see him, and tell him all that I owe him. He was living when I was here before, but, you know, at that time I was travelling with the Johnsons, who are not aesthetic, and who used to make me feel rather ashamed of my artistic temperament. If I had gone to see the great apostle of beauty, I should have had to go clandestinely – *en cachette*, as they say here – and that is not my nature; I like to do everything frankly, freely, *naïvement, au grand jour*. That is the great thing – to be free, to be frank, to be *naïf*. Doesn't Matthew Arnold say that somewhere – or is it Swinburne, or Pater?

When I was with the Johnsons everything was superficial; and, as regards life, everything was brought down to the question of right and wrong. They were too didactic; art should never be didactic, and what is life but an art? Pater has said that so well, somewhere. With the Johnsons I am afraid I lost many opportunities; the tone was gray and cottony, I might almost say woolly. But now, as I tell you, I have determined to take right hold for myself; to look right into European life, and judge it without Johnsonian prejudices. I have taken up my residence in a French family, in a real Parisian house. You see I have the courage of my opinions; I don't shrink from carrying out my theory that the great thing is to *live*.

You know I have always been intensely interested in Balzac, who never shrank from the reality, and whose almost *lurid* pictures of Parisian life have often haunted me in my wanderings through the old wicked-looking streets on the other side of the river. I am only sorry that my new friends – my French family – do not live in the old city – *au coeur du vieux Paris*, as they say here. They live only in the Boulevard Haussman, which is less picturesque; but in spite of this they have a great deal of the Balzac tone. Madame de Maisonrouge belongs to one of the oldest and proudest families in France; but she has had reverses which have compelled her to open an establishment in which a limited number of travellers, who are weary of the beaten track, who have the sense of local colour – she explains it herself, she expresses it so well –

in short, to open a sort of boarding house. I don't see why I should not, after all, use that expression, for it is the correlative of the term *pension bourgeoise*, employed by Balzac in the *Père Goriot*. Do you remember the *pension bourgeoise* of Mme Vauquer *née* de Conflans? But this establishment is not at all like that: and indeed it is not at all *bourgeois*; there is something distinguished, something aristocratic, about it. The Pension Vauquer was dark, brown, sordid, *graisseuse*; but this is in quite a different tone, with high, clear, lightly-draped windows, tender, subtle, almost morbid, colours, and furniture in elegant, studied, reed-like lines. Madame de Maisonrouge reminds me of Madame Hulot – do you remember 'la belle Mme Hulot'? – in *Les Parents Pauvres*. She has a great charm; a little artificial, a little fatigued, with a little suggestion of hidden things in her life; but I have always been sensitive to the charm of fatigue, of duplicity.

I am rather disappointed, I confess, in the society I find here; it is not so local, so characteristic, as I could have desired. Indeed, to tell the truth, it is not local at all; but, on the other hand, it is cosmopolitan, and there is a great advantage in that. We are French, we are English, we are American, we are German; and, I believe, there are some Russians and Hungarians expected. I am much interested in the study of national types; in comparing, contrasting, seizing the strong points, the weak points, the point of view of each. It is interesting to shift one's point of view – to enter into strange, exotic ways of looking at life.

The American types here are not, I am sorry to say, so interesting as they might be, and, excepting myself, are exclusively feminine. We are *thin*, my dear Harvard, we are pale, we are sharp. There is something meagre about us; our line is wanting in roundness, our composition in richness. We lack temperament; we don't know how to live; *nous ne savons pas vivre*, as they say here. The American temperament is represented (putting myself aside, and I often think that my temperament is not at all American) by a young girl and her mother, and another young girl without her mother – without her mother or any attendant or appendage whatever. These young girls are rather curious types; they have a certain interest, they have a certain grace, but they are disappointing too; they don't go far; they don't keep all they promise; they don't satisfy the imagination. They are cold, slim, sexless; the physique is not generous, not abundant; it is only the drapery, the skirts and furbelows (that is, I mean, in the young lady who has her mother) that are abundant. They are very different: one of them all elegance, all expensiveness, with an air of high fashion, from New York; the other a plain, pure, clear-eyed, straight-waisted, straight-stepping maiden from the heart of New England. And yet they are very much alike too – more alike than they would care to think themselves, for they eye each other with cold, mistrustful, deprecating looks. They are both specimens of the emancipated young American girl – practical, positive, passionless, subtle, and knowing, as you please, either too much or too little. And yet, as I say, they have a certain stamp, a certain grace. I like to talk with them, to study them.

The fair New Yorker is, sometimes, very amusing; she asks me if everyone in Boston talks like me – if everyone is as 'intellectual' as your poor correspondent. She is for ever throwing Boston up at me; I can't get rid of Boston. The other one rubs it into me too, but in a different way; she seems to feel about it as a good Mahommedan feels towards Mecca, and regards it as a kind of focus of light for the whole human race. Poor little Boston, what nonsense is talked in thy name! But this New England maiden is, in her way, a strange type: she is travelling all over Europe alone – 'to see it,' she says, 'for herself.' For herself! What can that stiff, slim self of hers do with such sights, such visions! She looks at everything, goes everywhere, passes her way, with her clear quiet eyes wide open; skirting the edge of obscene abysses without suspecting them; pushing through brambles without tearing her robe; exciting, without knowing it, the most injurious suspicions; and always holding her course, passionless, stainless, fearless, charmless! It is a little figure in which, after all, if you can get the right point of view, there is something rather striking.

By way of contrast, there is a lovely English girl, with eyes as shy as violets, and a voice as sweet! She has a sweet Gainsborough head, and a great Gainsborough hat, with a mighty plume in front of it, which makes a shadow over her quiet English eyes. Then she has a sage-green robe, 'mystic, wonderful', all embroidered with subtle devices and flowers, and birds of tender tint; very straight and tight in front, and adorned behind, along the spine, with large, strange, iridescent buttons. The revival of taste, of the sense of beauty, in England, interests me deeply; what is there in a simple row of spinal buttons to make one dream – to *donner à rêver*, as they say here? I think that a great aesthetic renascence is at hand, and that a great light will be kindled in England, for all the world to see. There are spirits there that I should like to commune with; I think they would understand me.

This gracious English maiden, with her clinging robes, her amulets and girdles, with something quaint and angular in her step, her carriage something mediaeval and Gothic, in the details of her person and dress, this lovely Evelyn Vane (isn't it a beautiful name?) is deeply, delightfully picturesque. She is much a woman – *elle est bien femme*, as they say here; simpler, softer, rounder, richer than the young girls I spoke of just now. Not much talk – a great, sweet silence. Then the violet eye – the very eye itself seems to blush; the great shadowy hat, making the brow so quiet; the strange, clinging, clutching, pictured raiment! As I say, it is a very gracious, tender type. She has her brother with her, who is a beautiful, fair-haired, gray-eyed young Englishman. He is purely objective; and he, too, is very plastic.

V

From MIRANDA HOPE *to her* MOTHER
September 26th

You must not be frightened at not hearing from me oftener; it is not because I am in any trouble, but because I am getting on so well. If I were in any trouble I don't think I should write to you; I should just keep quiet and see it through myself. But that is not the case at present; and, if I don't write to you, it is because I am so deeply interested over here that I don't seem to find time. It was a real providence that brought me to this house, where, in spite of all obstacles, I am able to do much good work. I wonder how I find the time for all I do; but when I think that I have only got a year in Europe, I feel as if I wouldn't sacrifice a single hour.

The obstacles I refer to are the disadvantages I have in learning French, there being so many persons around me speaking English, and that, as you may say, in the very bosom of a French family. It seems as if you heard English everywhere; but I certainly didn't expect to find it in a place like this. I am not discouraged, however, and I talk French all I can, even with the other English boarders. Then I have a lesson every day from Miss Maisonrouge (the elder daughter of the lady of the house), and French conversation every evening in the *salon*, from eight to eleven, with Madame herself, and some friends of hers that often come in. Her cousin, Mr Verdier, a young French gentleman, is fortunately staying with her, and I make a point of talking with him as much as possible. I have *extra private lessons* from him, and I often go out to walk with him. Some night, soon, he is to accompany me to the opera. We have also a most interesting plan of visiting all the galleries in Paris together. Like most of the French, he converses with great fluency, and I feel as if I should really gain from him. He is remarkably handsome, and extremely polite – paying a great many compliments, which, I am afraid, are not always *sincere*. When I return to Bangor I will tell you some of the things he has said to me. I think you will consider them extremely curious, and very beautiful *in their way*.

The conversation in the parlour (from eight to eleven) is often remarkably brilliant, and I often wish that you, or some of the Bangor folks, could be there to enjoy it. Even though you couldn't understand it I think you would like to hear the way they go on; they seem to express so much. I sometimes think that at Bangor they don't express enough (but it seems as if over there, there was less to express). It seems as if, at Bangor, there were things that folks never *tried* to say; but here, I have learned from studying French that you have no idea what you *can* say, before you try. At Bangor they seem to give it up beforehand; they don't make any effort. (I don't say this in the least for William Platt, *in particular*.)

I am sure I don't know what they will think of me when I get back. It seems as if, over here, I had learned to come out with everything. I suppose they will think I am not sincere; but isn't it more sincere to come out with things than to conceal them? I have become very good friends with everyone in the house – that is (you see, I *am* sincere), with *almost* everyone. It is the most interesting circle I ever was in. There's a girl here, an American, that I don't like so much as the rest; but that is only because she won't let me. I should like to like her, ever so much, because she is most lovely and most attractive; but she doesn't seem to want to know me or to like me. She comes from New York, and she is remarkably pretty, with beautiful eyes and the most delicate features; she is also remarkably elegant – in this respect would bear comparison with anyone I have seen over here. But it seems as if she didn't want to recognise me or associate with me; as if she wanted to make a difference between us. It is like people they call 'haughty' in books. I have never seen anyone like that before – anyone that wanted to make a differ-ence; and at first I was right down interested, she seemed to me so like a proud young lady in a novel. I kept saying to myself all day, 'haughty, haughty,' and I wished she would keep on so. But she did keep on; she kept on too long; and then I began to feel hurt. I couldn't think what I have done, and I can't think yet. It's as if she had got some idea about me, or had heard someone say something. If some girls should behave like that I shouldn't make any account of it, but this one is so refined, and looks as if she might be so interesting if I once got to know her, that I think about it a good deal. I am bound to find out what her reason is – for of course she has got some reason; I am right down curious to know.

I went up to her to ask her the day before yesterday; I thought that was the best way. I told her I wanted to know her better, and would like to come and see her in her room – they tell me she has got a lovely room – and that if she had heard anything against me, perhaps she would tell me when I came. But she was more distant than ever, and she just turned it off; said that she had never heard me mentioned, and that her room was too small to receive visitors. I suppose she spoke the truth, but I am sure she has got some reason, all the same. She has got some idea, and I am bound to find out before I go, if I have to ask everybody in the house. I *am* right down curious. I wonder if she doesn't think me refined – or if she had ever heard anything against Bangor? I can't think it is that. Don't you remember when Clara Barnard went to visit New York, three years ago, how much attention she received? And you know Clara *is* Bangor, to the soles of her shoes. Ask William Platt – so long as he isn't a native – if he doesn't consider Clara Barnard refined.

Apropos, as they say here, of refinement, there is another American in the house – a gentleman from Boston – who is just crowded with it. His name is Mr Louis Leverett (such a beautiful name, I think), and he is about thirty years old. He is rather small, and he looks pretty sick; he suffers from some affection of the liver. But his conversation is remarkably interesting, and I delight to listen to him – he has such beautiful ideas. I feel as if it were hardly right, not being in French; but, fortunately, he uses a great many French expressions. It's in a different style from the conversation of Mr Verdier – not so complimentary, but more intellectual. He is intensely fond of pictures, and has given me a great many ideas about them which I should never have gained without him; I shouldn't have known where to look for such ideas. He thinks everything of pictures; he thinks we don't make near enough of them. They seem to make a good deal of them here; but I couldn't help telling him the other day that in Bangor I really don't think we do.

If I had any money to spend I would buy some and take them back, to hang up. Mr Leverett says it would do them good – not the pictures, but the Bangor folks. He thinks everything of the French, too, and says we don't make nearly enough of *them*. I couldn't help telling him the other day that at any rate they make enough of themselves. But it is very interesting to hear him go on about the French, and it is so much gain to me, so long as that is what I came for. I talk to him as much as I dare about Boston, but I do feel as if this were right down wrong – a stolen pleasure.

I can get all the Boston culture I want when I go back, if I carry out my plan, my happy vision, of going there to reside. I ought to direct all my efforts to European culture now, and keep Boston to finish off. But it seems as if I couldn't help taking a peep now and then, in advance – with a Bostonian. I don't know when I may meet one again; but if there are many others like Mr Leverett there, I shall be certain not to want when I carry out my dream. He is just as full of culture as he can live. But it seems strange how many different sorts there are.

There are two of the English who I suppose are very cultivated too; but it doesn't seem as if I could enter into theirs so easily, though I try all I can. I do love their way of speaking, and sometimes I feel almost as if it would be right to give up trying to learn French, and just try to learn to speak our own tongue as these English speak it. It isn't the things they say so much, though these are often rather curious, but it is in the way they pronounce, and the sweetness of their voice. It seems as if they must *try* a good deal to talk like that, but these English that are here don't seem to try at all, either to speak or do anything else. They are a young lady and her brother. I believe they belong to some noble family. I have had a good deal of intercourse with them, because I have felt more free to talk to them than to the Americans – on account of the language. It seems as if in talking with them I was almost learning a new one.

I never supposed, when I left Bangor, that I was coming to Europe to learn *English*! If I do learn it, I don't think you will understand me when I get back, and I don't think you'll like it much. I should be a good deal criticised if I spoke like that at Bangor. However, I verily believe Bangor is the most critical place on earth; I have seen nothing like it over here. Tell them all I have come to the conclusion that they are *a great deal too fastidious*. But I was speaking about this English young lady and her brother. I wish I could put them before you. She is lovely to look at; she seems so modest and retiring. In spite of this, however, she dresses in a way that attracts great attention, as I couldn't help noticing when one day I went out to walk with her. She was ever so much looked at; but she didn't seem to notice it, until at last I couldn't help calling attention to it. Mr Leverett thinks everything of it; he calls it the 'costume of the future'. I should call it rather the costume of the past – you know the English have such an attachment to the past. I said this the other day to Mme de Maisonrouge – that Miss Vane dressed in the costume of the past. *De l'an passé, vous voulez dire?* said Madame, with her little French laugh (you can get William Platt to translate this, he used to tell me he knew so much French).

You know I told you, in writing some time ago, that I had tried to get some insight into the position of woman in England, and, being here with Miss Vane, it has seemed to me to be a good opportunity to get a little more. I have asked her a great deal about it; but she doesn't seem able to give me much information. The first time I asked her she told me the position of a lady depended upon the rank of her father, her eldest brother, her husband, etc. She told me her own position was very good, because her father was some relation – I forget what – to a lord. She thinks everything of this; and that proves to me that the position of woman in her country cannot be satisfactory; because, if it were, it wouldn't depend upon that of your relations, even your nearest. I don't know much about lords, and it does try my patience (though she is just as sweet as she can live) to hear her talk as if it were a matter of course that I should.

I feel as if it were right to ask her as often as I can if she doesn't consider everyone equal; but she always says she doesn't, and she confesses that she doesn't think she is equal to 'Lady Something-or-other', who is the wife of that relation of her father. I try and persuade her all I can that she is; but it seems as if she didn't want to be persuaded; and when I ask her if Lady So-and-so is of the same opinion (that Miss Vane isn't her equal), she looks so soft and pretty with her eyes, and says, 'Of course she is!' When I tell her that this is right down bad for Lady So-and-so, it seems as if she wouldn't believe me, and the only answer she will make is that Lady So-and-so is 'extremely nice'. I don't believe she is nice at all; if she were nice, she wouldn't have such ideas as that. I tell Miss Vane that at Bangor we think such ideas vulgar; but then she looks as though she had never heard of Bangor. I often want to shake her, though she *is* so sweet. If she isn't angry with the people who make her feel that way, I am angry for her. I am angry with her brother too, for she is evidently very much afraid of him, and this gives me some further insight into the subject. She thinks everything of her brother, and thinks it natural that she should be afraid of him, not only physically (for this *is* natural, as he is enormously tall and strong, and has very big fists), but morally and intellectually. She seems unable, however, to take in any argument, and she makes me realise what I have often heard – that if you are timid nothing will reason you out of it.

Mr Vane, also (the brother), seems to have the same prejudices, and when I tell him, as I often think it right to do, that his sister is not his subordinate, even if she does think so, but his equal, and, perhaps in some respects his superior, and that if my brother, in Bangor, were to treat me as he treats this poor young girl, who has not spirit enough to see the question in its true light, there would be an indignation-meeting of the citizens, to protest against such an outrage to the sanctity of womanhood – when I tell him all this, at breakfast or dinner, he bursts out laughing so loud that all the plates clatter on the table.

But at such a time as this there is always one person who seems interested in what I say – a German gentleman, a professor, who sits next to me at dinner, and whom I must tell you more about another time. He is very learned, and has a great desire for information; he appreciates a great many of my remarks, and, after dinner, in the salon, he often comes to me to ask me questions about them. I have to think a little, sometimes, to know what I did say, or what I do think. He takes you right up where you left off, and he is almost as fond of discussing things as William Platt is. He is splendidly educated, in the German style, and he told me the other day that he was an 'intellectual broom'. Well, if he is, he sweeps clean; I told him that. After he has been talking to me I feel as if I hadn't got a speck of dust left in my mind anywhere. It's a most delightful feeling. He says he's an observer; and I am sure there is plenty over here to observe. But I have told you enough for today. I don't know how much longer I shall stay here; I am getting on so fast that it sometimes seems as if I shouldn't need all the time I have laid out. I suppose your cold weather has promptly begun, as usual; it sometimes makes me envy you. The fall weather here is very dull and damp, and I feel very much as if I should like to be braced up.

VI
From MISS EVELYN VANE, *in Paris,*
to the LADY AUGUSTA FLEMING, *at Brighton*
Paris, September 30th

Dear Lady Augusta – I am afraid I shall not be able to come to you on January 7th, as you kindly proposed at Homburg. I am so very, very sorry; it is a great disappointment to me. But I have just heard that it has been settled that mamma and the children are coming abroad for a part of the winter, and mamma wishes me to go with them to Hyères, where Georgina has been ordered for her lungs. She has not been at all well these three months, and now that the damp weather has begun she is very poorly indeed; so that last week papa decided to have a consultation, and he and mamma went with her up to town and saw some three or four doctors. They all of them ordered the south of France, but they didn't agree about the place; so that mamma herself decided for Hyères, because it is the most economical. I believe it is very dull, but I hope it will do Georgina good. I am afraid, however, that nothing will do her good until she consents to take more care of herself; I am afraid she is very wild and wilful, and mamma tells me that all this month it has taken papa's positive orders to make her stop indoors. She is very cross (mamma writes me) about coming abroad, and doesn't seem at all to mind the expense that papa has been put to – talks very ill-naturedly about losing the hunting, etc. She expected to begin to hunt in December, and wants to know whether anybody keeps hounds at Hyères. Fancy a girl wanting to follow the hounds when her lungs are so bad! But I daresay that when she gets there she will be glad enough to keep quiet, as they say that the heat is intense. It may cure Georgina, but I am sure it will make the rest of us very ill.

Mamma, however, is only going to bring Mary and Gus and Fred and Adelaide abroad with her; the others will remain at Kingscote until February (about the 3rd), when they will go to Eastbourne for a month with Miss Turnover, the new governess, who has turned out such a very nice person. She is going to take Miss Travers, who has been with us so long, but who is only qualified for the younger children, to Hyères, and I believe some of the Kingscote servants. She has perfect confidence in Miss T.; it is only a pity she has such an odd name. Mamma thought of asking her if she would mind taking another when she came; but papa thought she might object. Lady Battledown makes all her governesses take the same name. She gives £5 more a year for the purpose. I forget what it is she calls them. I think it's Johnson (which to me always suggests a lady's maid). Governesses shouldn't have too pretty a name; they shouldn't have a nicer name than the family.

I suppose you heard from the Desmonds that I did not go back to England with them. When it began to be talked about that Georgina should be taken abroad, mamma wrote to me that I had better stop in Paris for a month with Harold, so that she could pick me up on their way to Hyères. It saves the expense of my journey to Kingscote and back, and gives me the opportunity to 'finish' a little in French.

You know Harold came here six weeks ago, to get up his French for those dreadful examinations that he has to pass so soon. He came to live with some French people that take in young men (and others) for this purpose; it's a kind of coaching place, only kept by women. Mamma had heard it was very nice; so she wrote to me that I was to come and stop here with Harold. The Desmonds brought me and made the arrangement, or the bargain, or whatever you call it. Poor Harold was naturally not at all pleased; but he has been very kind, and has treated me like an angel. He is getting on beautifully with his French; for though I don't think the place is so good as papa supposed, yet Harold is so immensely clever that he can scarcely help learning. I am afraid I learn much less, but, fortunately, I have not to pass an examination – except if mamma takes it into her head to examine me. But she will have so much to think of with Georgina that I hope this won't occur to her. If it does, I shall be, as Harold says, in a dreadful funk.

This is not such a nice place for a girl as for a young man, and the Desmonds thought it *exceedingly odd* that mamma should wish me to come here. As Mrs Desmond said, it is because she is so very unconventional. But you know Paris is so very amusing, and if only Harold remains good-natured about it, I shall be content to wait for the caravan (that's what he calls mamma and the children). The person who keeps the establishment, or whatever they call it, is rather odd, and *exceedingly foreign*; but she is wonderfully civil, and is perpetually sending to my door to see if I want anything. The servants are not at all like English servants, and come bursting in, the footman (they have only one) and the maids alike, at all sorts of hours, in the *most sudden way*. Then when one rings, it is half an hour before they come. All this is very uncomfortable, and I daresay it will be worse at Hyères. There, however, fortunately, we shall have our own people.

There are some very odd Americans here, who keep throwing Harold into fits of laughter. One is a dreadful little man who is always sitting over the fire, and talking about the colour of the sky. I don't believe he ever saw the sky except through the windowpane. The other day he took hold of my frock (that green one you thought so nice at Homburg) and told me that it reminded him of the texture of the

Devonshire turf. And then he talked for half an hour about the Devonshire turf, which I thought such a very extraordinary subject. Harold says he is mad. It is very strange to be living in this way with people one doesn't know. I mean that one doesn't know as one knows them in England.

The other Americans (beside the madman) are two girls, about my own age, one of whom is rather nice. She has a mother, but the mother is always sitting in her bedroom, which seems so very odd. I should like mamma to ask them to Kingscote, but I am afraid mamma wouldn't like the mother, who is rather vulgar. The other girl is rather vulgar too, and is travelling about quite alone. I think she is a kind of school-mistress; but the other girl (I mean the nicer one, with the mother) tells me she is more respectable than she seems. She has, however, the most extraordinary opinions – wishes to do away with the aristocracy, thinks it wrong that Arthur should have Kingscote when papa dies, etc. I don't see what it signifies to her that poor Arthur should come into the property, which will be so delightful – except for papa dying. But Harold says she is mad. He chaffs her tremendously about her radicalism, and he is so immensely clever that she can't answer him, though she is rather clever too.

There is also a Frenchman, a nephew, or cousin, or something, of the person of the house, who is extremely nasty; and a German professor, or doctor, who eats with his knife and is a great bore. I am so very sorry about giving up my visit. I am afraid you will never ask me again.

VII
From LÉON VERDIER, *in Paris,*
to PROSPER GOBAIN, *at Lille*
September 28th

MY DEAR PROSPER –

It is a long time since I have given you of my news, and I don't know what puts it into my head tonight to recall myself to your affectionate memory. I suppose it is that when we are happy the mind reverts instinctively to those with whom formerly we shared our exaltations and depressions, and *je t'en ai trop dit, dans le bon temps, mon gros Prosper*, and you always listened to me too imperturbably, with your pipe in your mouth, your waistcoat unbuttoned, for me not to feel that I can count upon your sympathy today. *Nous en sommes nous flanquées, des confidences* – in those happy days when my first thought in seeing an adventure *poindre à l'horizon* was of the pleasure I should have in relating it to the great Prosper. As I tell thee, I am happy; decidedly, I am happy, and from this affirmation I fancy you can construct the rest. Shall I help thee a little? Take three adorable girls… three, my good Prosper – the mystic number – neither more nor less. Take them and place thy insatiable little Léon in the midst of them! Is the situation sufficiently indicated, and do you apprehend the motives of my felicity?

You expected, perhaps, I was going to tell you that I had made my fortune, or that the Uncle Blondeau had at last decided to return into the breast of nature, after having constituted me his universal legatee. But I needn't remind you that women are always for something in the happiness of him who writes to thee – for something in his happiness, and for a good deal more in his misery. But don't let me talk of misery now; time enough when it comes; *ces demoiselles* have gone to join the serried ranks of their amiable predecessors. Excuse me – I comprehend your impatience. I will tell you of whom *ces demoiselles* consist.

You have heard me speak of my *cousine* de Maisonrouge, that *grande belle femme*, who, after having married, *en secondes noces* – there had been, to tell the truth, some irregularity about her first union – a venerable relic of the old noblesse of Poitou, was left, by the death of her husband, complicated by the indulgence of expensive tastes on an income of 17,000 francs, on the pavement of Paris, with two little demons of daughters to bring up in the path of virtue. She managed to bring them up; my little cousins are rigidly virtuous. If you ask me how she managed it, I can't tell you; it's no business of mine, and, *à fortiori*, none of yours. She is now fifty years old (she confesses to thirty-seven), and her daughters, whom she has never been able to marry, are respectively twenty-seven and twenty-three (they confess to twenty and to seventeen). Three years ago she had the thrice-blessed idea of opening a sort of *pension* for the entertainment and instruction of the blundering barbarians who come to Paris in the hope of picking up a few stray particles of the language of Voltaire – or of Zola. The idea *lui a porté bonheur*; the shop does a very good business. Until within a few months ago it was carried on by my cousins alone, but lately the need of a few extensions and embellishments has caused itself to be felt. My cousin has undertaken them, regardless of expense; she has asked me to come and stay with her – board and lodging gratis – and keep an eye on the grammatical eccentricities of her *pensionnaires*. I am the extension, my good Prosper, I am the embellishment! I live for nothing, and I straighten up the accent of the prettiest English lips. The English lips are not all pretty, heaven knows, but enough of them are so to make it a gaining bargain for me.

Just now, as I told you, I am in daily conversation with three separate pairs. The owner of one of them has private lessons; she pays extra. My cousin doesn't give me a sou of the money; but I make bold, nevertheless, to say that my trouble is remunerated. But I am well, very well, with the proprietors of the two other pairs. One of them is a little Anglaise, of about twenty – a little *figure de keepsake*; the most adorable miss that you ever, or at least that I ever, beheld. She is decorated all over with beads and bracelets and embroidered dandelions; but her principal decoration consists of the softest little gray eyes in the world, which rest upon you with a profundity of confidence – a confidence that I really feel some compunction in betraying. She has a tint as white as this sheet of paper, except just in the middle of each cheek, where it passes into the purest and most transparent, most liquid, carmine. Occasionally this rosy fluid overflows into the rest of her face – by which I mean that she blushes – as softly as the mark of your breath on the windowpane.

Like every Anglaise, she is rather pinched and prim in public; but it is very easy to see that when no one is looking *elle ne demande qu'à se laisser aller*! Whenever she wants it I am always there, and I have given her to understand that she can count upon me. I have every reason to believe that she appreciates the assurance, though I am bound in honesty to confess that with her the situation is a little less advanced than with the others. *Que voulez-vous?* The English are heavy, and the Anglaises move slowly, that's all. The movement, however, is perceptible, and once this fact is established I can let the pottage simmer.

I can give her time to arrive, for I am over-well occupied with her *concurrentes. Celles-ci* don't keep me waiting, *par exemple*!

These young ladies are Americans, and you know that it is the national character to move fast. 'All right – go ahead!' (I am learning a great deal of English, or, rather, a great deal of American.) They go ahead at a rate that sometimes makes it difficult for me to keep up. One of them is prettier than the other; but this latter (the one that takes the private lessons) is really *une fille prodigieuse. Ah, par exemple, elle brûle ses vaisseux cella-là*! She threw herself into my arms the very first day, and I almost owed her a grudge for having deprived me of that pleasure of gradation, of carrying the defences, one by one, which is almost as great as that of entering the place.

Would you believe that at the end of exactly twelve minutes she gave me a rendezvous? It is true it was in the Galerie d'Apollon, at the Louvre; but that was respectable for a beginning, and since then we have had them by the dozen; I have ceased to keep the account. *Non, c'est une fille qui me dépasse.*

The little one (she has a mother somewhere, out of sight, shut up in a closet or a trunk) is a good deal prettier, and, perhaps, on that account *elle y met plus de façons*. She doesn't knock about Paris with me by the hour; she contents herself with long interviews in the *petit salon*, with the curtains half-drawn, beginning at about three o'clock, when everyone is *à la promenade*. She is admirable, this little one; a little too thin, the bones rather accentuated, but the detail, on the whole, most satisfactory. And you can say anything to her. She takes the trouble to appear not to understand, but her conduct, half an hour afterwards, reassures you completely – oh, completely!

However, it is the tall one, the one of the private lessons, that is the most remarkable. These private lessons, my good Prosper, are the most brilliant invention of the age, and a real stroke of genius on the part of Miss Miranda! They also take place in the *petit salon*, but with the doors tightly closed, and with explicit directions to everyone in the house that we are not to be disturbed. And we are not, my good Prosper, we are not! Not a sound, not a shadow, interrupts our felicity. My *cousine* is really admirable; the shop deserves to succeed. Miss Miranda is tall and rather flat; she is too pale; she hasn't the adorable *rougeurs* of the little Anglaise. But she has bright, keen, inquisitive eyes, superb teeth, a nose modelled by a sculptor, and a way of holding up her head and looking everyone in the face, which is the most finished piece of impertinence I ever beheld. She is making the *tour du monde* entirely alone, without even a soubrette to carry the ensign, for the purpose of seeing for herself *à quoi s'en tenir sur les hommes et les choses* – on *les hommes* particularly. *Dis donc*, Prosper, it must be a *drôle de pays* over there, where young persons animated by this ardent curiosity are manufactured! If we should turn the tables, some day, thou and I, and go over and see it for ourselves. It is as well that we should go and find them *chez elles*, as that they should come out here after us. *Dis donc, mon gras Prosper…*

VIII
From DR RUDOLF STAUB, *in Paris,* *to* DR JULIUS HIRSCH, *at Göttingen*

MY DEAR BROTHER IN SCIENCE –

I resume my hasty notes, of which I sent you the first instalment some weeks ago. I mentioned then that I intended to leave my hotel, not finding it sufficiently local and national. It was kept by a Pomeranian, and the waiters, without exception, were from the Fatherland. I fancied myself at Berlin, Unter den Linden, and I reflected that, having taken the serious step of visiting the headquarters of the Gallic genius, I should try and project myself, as much as possible, into the circumstances which are in part the consequence and in part the cause of its irrepressible activity. It seemed to me that there could be no well-grounded knowledge without this preliminary operation of placing myself in relations, as slightly as possible modified by elements proceeding from a different combination of causes, with the spontaneous home-life of the country.

I accordingly engaged a room in the house of a lady of pure French extraction and education, who supplements the shortcomings of an income insufficient to the ever-growing demands of the Parisian system of sense-gratification, by providing food and lodging for a limited number of distinguished strangers. I should have preferred to have my room alone in the house, and to take my meals in a brewery, of very good appearance, which I speedily discovered in the same street; but this arrangement, though very lucidly proposed by myself, was not acceptable to the mistress of the establishment (a woman with a mathematical head), and I have consoled myself for the extra expense by fixing my thoughts upon the opportunity that conformity to the customs of the house gives me of studying the table manners of my companions, and of observing the French nature at a peculiarly physiological moment, the moment when the satisfaction of the *taste*, which is the governing quality in its composition, produces a kind of exhalation, an intellectual transpiration, which, though light and perhaps invisible to a superficial spectator, is nevertheless appreciable by a properly adjusted instrument.

I have adjusted my instrument very satisfactorily (I mean the one I carry in my good square German head), and I am not afraid of losing a single drop of this valuable fluid, as it condenses itself upon the plate of my observation. A prepared surface is what I need, and I have prepared my surface.

Unfortunately here, also, I find the individual native in the minority. There are only four French persons in the house – the individuals concerned in its management, three of whom are women, and one a man. This preponderance of the feminine element is, however, in itself characteristic, as I need not remind you what an abnormally-developed part this sex has played in French history. The remaining figure is apparently that of a man, but I hesitate to classify him so super-ficially. He appears to me less human than simian, and whenever I hear him talk I seem to myself to have paused in the street to listen to the shrill clatter of a hand-organ, to which the gambols of a hairy *homunculus* form an accompaniment.

I mentioned to you before that my expectation of rough usage, in consequence of my German nationality, had proved completely unfounded. No one seems to know or to care what my nationality is, and I am treated, on the contrary, with the civility which is the portion of every traveller who pays the bill without scanning the items too narrowly. This, I confess, has been something of a surprise to me, and

I have not yet made up my mind as to the fundamental cause of the anomaly. My determination to take up my abode in a French interior was largely dictated by the supposition that I should be substantially disagreeable to its inmates. I wished to observe the different forms taken by the irritation that I should naturally produce. For it is under the influence of irritation that the French character most completely expresses itself. My presence, however, does not appear to operate as a stimulus, and in this respect I am materially disappointed. They treat me as they treat everyone else; whereas, in order to be treated differently, I was resigned in advance to be treated worse. I have not, as I say, fully explained to myself this logical contradiction. But this is the explanation to which I tend. The French are so exclusively occupied with the idea of themselves, that in spite of the very definite image the German personality presented to them by the war of 1870, they have at present no distinct apprehension of its existence. They are not very sure that there are any Germans; they have already forgotten the convincing proofs of the fact that were presented to them nine years ago. A German was something disagreeable, which they determined to keep out of their conception of things. I therefore think that we are wrong to govern ourselves upon the hypothesis of the *revanche*; the French nature is too shallow for that large and powerful plant to bloom in it.

The English-speaking specimens, too, I have not been willing to neglect the opportunity to examine; and among these I have paid special attention to the American varieties, of which I find here several singular examples. The two most remarkable are a young man who presents all the characteristics of a period of national decadence, reminding me strongly of some diminutive Hellenised Roman of the third century. He is an illustration of the period of culture in which the faculty of appreciation has obtained such a preponderance over that of production that the latter sinks into a kind of rank sterility, and the mental condition becomes analogous to that of a malarious bog. I learn from him that there is an immense number of Americans exactly resembling him, and that the city of Boston, indeed, is almost exclusively composed of them. (He communicated this fact very proudly, as if it were greatly to the credit of his native country, little perceiving the truly sinister impression it made upon me.)

What strikes one in it is that it is a phenomenon to the best of my knowledge – and you know what my knowledge is – unprecedented and unique in the history of mankind; the arrival of a nation at an ultimate stage of evolution without having passed through the mediate one; the passage of the fruit, in other words, from crudity to rottenness, without the interposition of a period of useful (and ornamental) ripeness. With the Americans, indeed, the crudity and the rottenness are identical and simultaneous; it is impossible to say, as in the conversation of this deplorable young man, which is one and which is the other; they are inextricably mingled. I prefer the talk of the French *homunculus*; it is at least more amusing.

It is interesting in this manner to perceive, so largely developed, the germs of extinction in the so-called powerful Anglo-Saxon family. I find them in almost as recognisable a form in a young woman from the State of Maine, in the province of New England, with whom I have had a good deal of conversation. She differs somewhat from the young man I just mentioned, in that the faculty of production, of action, is, in her, less inanimate; she has more of the freshness and vigour that we suppose to belong to a young civilisation. But unfortunately she produces nothing but evil, and her tastes and habits are similarly those of a Roman lady of the lower Empire. She makes no secret of them, and has, in fact, elaborated a complete system of licentious behaviour. As the opportunities she finds in her own country do not satisfy her, she has come to Europe 'to try,' as she says, 'for herself'. It is the doctrine of universal experience professed with a cynicism that is really most extraordinary, and which, presenting itself in a young woman of considerable education, appears to me to be the judgement of a society.

Another observation which pushes me to the same induction – that of the premature vitiation of the American population – is the attitude of the Americans whom I have before me with regard to each other. There is another young lady here, who is less abnormally developed than the one I have just described, but who yet bears the stamp of this peculiar combination of incompleteness and effeteness. These three persons look with the greatest mistrust and aversion upon each other; and each has repeatedly taken me apart and assured me, secretly, that he or she only is the real, the genuine, the typical

American. A type that has lost itself before it has been fixed – what can you look for from this?

Add to this that there are two young Englanders in the house, who hate all the Americans in a lump, making between them none of the distinctions and favourable comparisons which they insist upon, and you will, I think, hold me warranted in believing that, between precipitate decay and internecine enmities, the English-speaking family is destined to consume itself, and that with its decline the prospect of general pervasiveness, to which I alluded above, will brighten for the deep-lunged children of the Fatherland!

IX
MIRANDA HOPE
to her MOTHER
October 22nd

DEAR MOTHER –
I am off in a day or two to visit some new country; I haven't yet decided which. I have satisfied myself with regard to France, and obtained a good knowledge of the language. I have enjoyed my visit to Mme de Maisonrouge deeply, and feel as if I were leaving a circle of real friends. Everything has gone on beautifully up to the end, and everyone has been as kind and attentive as if I were their own sister, especially Mr Verdier, the French gentleman, from whom I have gained more than I ever expected (in six weeks), and with whom I have promised to *correspond*. So you can imagine me dashing off the most correct French letters; and, if you don't believe it, I will keep the rough draft to show you when I go back.

The German gentleman is also more interesting, the more you know him; it seems sometimes as if I could fairly drink in his ideas. I have found out why the young lady from New York doesn't like me! It is because I said one day at dinner that I *admired* to go to the Louvre. Well, when I first came, it seemed as if I *did* admire everything!

Tell William Platt his letter has come. I knew he would have to write, and I was bound I would make him! I haven't decided what country

I will visit yet; it seems as if there were so many to choose from. But I shall take care to pick out a good one, and to meet plenty of fresh experiences.

Dearest mother, my money holds out, and it *is* most interesting!

THE POINT OF VIEW

I

FROM MISS AURORA CHURCH, AT SEA,
TO MISS WHITESIDE, IN PARIS

... My dear child, the bromide of sodium (if that's what you call it) proved perfectly useless. I don't mean that it did me no good, but that I never had occasion to take the bottle out of my bag. It might have done wonders for me if I had needed it; but I didn't, simply because I have been a wonder myself. Will you believe that I have spent the whole voyage on deck, in the most animated conversation and exercise? Twelve times round the deck make a mile, I believe; and by this measurement I have been walking twenty miles a day. And down to every meal, if you please, where I have displayed the appetite of a fishwife. Of course the weather has been lovely; so there's no great merit. The wicked old Atlantic has been as blue as the sapphire in my only ring (a rather good one), and as smooth as the slippery floor of Madame Galopin's dining room. We have been for the last three hours in sight of land, and we are soon to enter the Bay of New York, which is said to be exquisitely beautiful. But of course you recall it, though they say that everything changes so fast over here. I find I don't remember anything, for my recollections of our voyage to Europe, so many years ago, are exceedingly dim; I only have a painful impression that mamma shut me up for an hour every day in the stateroom, and made me learn by heart some religious poem. I was only five years old, and I believe that as a child I was extremely timid; on the other hand, mamma, as you know, was dreadfully severe. She is severe to this day; only I have become indifferent; I have been so pinched and pushed – morally speaking, *bien entendu*. It is true, however, that there are children of five on the vessel today who have been extremely conspicuous – ranging all over the ship, and always under one's feet. Of course they are little compatriots, which means that they are little barbarians. I don't mean that all our compatriots are barbarous; they seem to improve, somehow, after their first communion. I don't know whether it's that ceremony that improves them, especially as so few of them go in for it; but the women are certainly nicer than the little girls; I mean, of course, in proportion, you know. You warned me not to generalise, and you see I have already begun, before we have arrived. But I suppose there is no harm in it so long as it is favourable. Isn't it favourable when I say that I have had the most lovely time? I have never had so much liberty in my life, and I have been out alone, as you may say, every day of the voyage. If it is a foretaste of what is to come, I shall take to that very kindly. When I say that I have been out alone, I mean that we have always been two. But we two were alone, so to speak, and it was not like always having mamma, or Madame Galopin, or some lady in the *pension*, or the temporary cook. Mamma has been very poorly; she is so very well on land, it's a wonder to see her at all taken down. She says, however, that it isn't the being at sea; it's, on the contrary, approaching the land. She is not in a hurry to arrive; she says that great disillusions await us. I didn't know that she had any illusions – she's so stern, so philosophic. She is very serious; she sits for hours in perfect silence, with her eyes fixed on the horizon. I heard her say yesterday to an English gentleman – a very odd Mr Antrobus, the only person with whom she converses – that she was afraid she shouldn't like her native land, and that she shouldn't like not liking it. But this is a mistake – she will like that immensely (I mean not liking it). If it should prove at all agreeable, mamma will be furious, for that will go against her system. You know all about mamma's system; I have explained that so often. It goes against her system that we should come back at all; that was *my* system – I have had at last to invent one! She consented to come only because she saw that, having no *dot*, I should never marry in Europe; and I pretended to be immensely preoccupied with this idea, in order to make her start. In reality *cela m'est parfaitement égal.* I am only afraid I shall like it too much (I don't mean marriage, of course, but one's native land). Say what you will, it's a charming thing to go out alone, and I have given notice to mamma that I mean to be always *en course*. When I tell her that, she looks at me in the same silence; her eye dilates, and then she slowly closes it. It's as if the sea were affecting her a little, though it's so beautifully calm. I ask her if she will try my bromide, which is there in my bag; but she motions me off, and I begin to walk again, tapping my little boot-soles upon the smooth clean deck. This allusion to my boot-soles, by the way, is not prompted by vanity; but it's a fact that at sea one's feet and one's shoes assume the most extraordinary importance, so that we should take the precaution to have nice ones. They are all you seem to see as the people walk about the deck; you get to know them intimately, and to dislike some of them so much. I am afraid you will think that I have already broken loose; and for aught I know, I am writing as a *demoiselle bien-elevée* should not write. I don't know whether it's the American air; if it is, all I can say is that the American air is very charming. It makes me impatient and restless, and I sit scribbling here because I am so eager to arrive, and the time passes better if I occupy myself. I am in the saloon, where we have our meals, and opposite to me is a big round porthole, wide open, to let in the smell of the land. Every now and then I rise a little and look through it, to see 5whether we are arriving. I mean in the Bay, you know, for we shall not come up to the city till dark. I don't want to lose the Bay; it appears that it's so wonderful. I don't exactly understand what it contains, except some beautiful islands; but I suppose you will know all about that. It is easy to see that these are the last hours, for all the people about me are writing letters to put into the post as soon as we come up to the dock. I believe they are dreadful at the custom-house, and you will remember how many new things you persuaded mamma that (with my preoccupation of marriage) I should take to this country, where even the prettiest girls are expected not to go unadorned. We ruined ourselves in Paris (that is part of mamma's solemnity); *mais au moins je serai belle*! Moreover, I believe that mamma is prepared to say or to do anything that may be necessary for escaping from their odious duties; as she very justly remarks, she can't afford to be ruined twice. I don't know how one approaches these terrible *douaniers*, but I mean to invent something very charming. I mean to say, '*Voyons, Messieurs*, a young girl like me, brought up in the strictest foreign traditions, kept always in the background by a very superior mother – *la voilà*; you can see for yourself! – what is it possible that she should attempt to smuggle in? Nothing but a few simple relics of her convent!' I won't tell them that my convent was called the *Magasin du Bon Marché*. Mamma began to scold me three days ago for insisting on so many trunks, and the truth is that, between us, we have not fewer than seven. For relics, that's a good many! We are all writing very long letters – or at least we are writing a great number. There is no news of the Bay as yet. Mr Antrobus, mamma's friend, opposite to me, is beginning on his ninth. He is an Honourable, and a Member of Parliament; he has written, during the voyage, about a hundred letters, and he seems greatly alarmed at the number of stamps he will have to buy when he arrives. He is full of information; but he has not enough, for he asks as many questions as mamma when she goes to hire apartments. He is going to 'look into' various things; he speaks as if they had a little hole for the purpose. He walks almost as much as I, and he has very big shoes. He asks questions even of me, and I tell him again and again that I know nothing about America. But it makes no difference; he always begins again, and, indeed, it is not strange that he should find my ignorance incredible. 'Now, how would it be in one of your South-Western States?' – that's his favourite way of opening conversation. Fancy me giving an account of the South-Western States! I tell him he had better ask mamma – a little to tease that lady, who knows no more about such places than I. Mr Antrobus is very big and black; he speaks with a sort of brogue; he has a wife and ten children; he is not very romantic. But he has lots of letters to people *là-bas* (I forget that we are just arriving), and mamma, who takes an interest in him in spite of his views (which are dreadfully advanced, and not at all like mamma's own), has promised to give him the *entrée* to the best society. I don't know what she knows about the best society over here today, for we have not kept up our connections at all, and no one will know (or, I am afraid, care) anything about us. She has an idea that we shall be immensely recognised. But really, except the poor little Rucks, who are bankrupt, and, I am told, in no society at all, I don't know on whom we can count. *C'est égal*. Mamma has an idea that, whether or not we appreciate America ourselves, we shall at least be universally appreciated. It's true that we have begun to be, a little; you would see that by the way that Mr Cockerel and Mr Louis Leverett are always inviting me to walk. Both of these gentlemen, who are Americans, have asked leave to call upon me in New York, and I have said, *Mon Dieu, oui*, if it's the custom of the country. Of course I have not dared to tell this to mamma, who flatters herself that we have brought with us in our trunks a complete set of customs of our own, and that we shall only have to shake them out a little and put them on when we arrive. If only the two gentlemen I just spoke of don't call at the same time, I don't think I shall be too much frightened. If they do, on the other hand, I won't answer for it. They have a particular aversion to each other, and they are ready to fight about poor little me. I am only the pretext, however, for, as Mr Leverett says, it's really the opposition of temperaments. I hope they won't cut each other's throats, for I am not crazy about either of them. They are very well for the deck of a ship, but I shouldn't care about them in a *salon*. They are not at all distinguished. They think they are, but they are not; at least Mr Louis Leverett does; Mr Cockerel doesn't appear to care so much. They are extremely different (with their opposed temperaments), and each very amusing for a while; but I should get dreadfully tired of passing my life with either. Neither has proposed that, as yet; but it is evidently what they are coming to. It will be in a great measure to spite each other, for I think that *au fond* they don't quite believe in me. If they don't, it's the only point on which they agree. They hate each other awfully; they take such different views. That is, Mr Cockerel hates Mr Leverett – he calls him a sickly little ass; he says that his opinions are half affectation, and the other half dyspepsia. Mr Leverett speaks of Mr Cockerel as a 'strident savage', but he declares he finds him most diverting. He says there is nothing in which we can't find a certain entertainment, if we only look at it in the right way, and that we have no business with either hating or loving; we ought only to strive to understand. To understand is to forgive, he says. That is very pretty, but I don't like the suppression of our affections, though I have no desire to fix mine upon Mr Leverett. He is very artistic, and talks like an article in some review. He has lived a great deal in Paris, and Mr Cockerel says that is what has made him such an idiot. That is not complimentary to you, dear Louisa, and still less to your brilliant brother, for Mr Cockerel explains that he means it (the bad effect of Paris) chiefly of the men. In fact, he means the bad effect of Europe altogether. This, however, is compromising to mamma; and I am afraid there is no doubt that (from what I have told him) he thinks mamma also an idiot. (I am not responsible, you know – I have always wanted to go home.) If mamma knew him, which she doesn't, for she always closes her eyes when I pass on his arm, she would think him disgusting. Mr Leverett, however, tells me he is nothing to what we shall see yet. He is from Philadelphia (Mr Cockerel); he insists that we shall go and see Philadelphia, but mamma says she saw it in 1855, and it was then *affreux*. Mr Cockerel says that mamma is evidently not familiar with the march of improvement in this country; he speaks of 1855 as if it were a hundred years ago. Mamma says she knows it goes only too fast – it goes so fast that it has time to do nothing well; and then Mr Cockerel, who, to do him justice, is perfectly good-natured, remarks that she had better wait till she has been ashore and seen the improvements. Mamma rejoins that she sees them from here, the improvements, and that they give her a sinking of the heart. (This little exchange of ideas is carried on through me; they have never spoken to each other.) Mr Cockerel, as I say, is extremely good-natured, and he carries out what I have heard said about the men in America being very considerate of the women. They evidently listen to them a great deal; they don't contradict them; but it seems to me that this is rather negative. There is very little gallantry in not contradicting one; and it strikes me that there are some things the men don't express. There are others on the ship whom I've noticed. It's as if they were all one's brothers or one's cousins. But I promised you not to generalise, and perhaps there will be more expression when we arrive. Mr Cockerel returns to America, after a general tour, with a renewed conviction that this is the only country. I left him on deck an hour ago looking at the coastline with an opera glass, and saying it was the prettiest thing he had seen in all his tour. When I remarked that the coast seemed rather low, he said it would be all the easier to get ashore; Mr Leverett doesn't seem in a hurry to get ashore; he is sitting within sight of me in a corner of the saloon – writing letters, I suppose, but looking, from the way he bites his pen and rolls his eyes about, as if he were composing a sonnet and waiting for a rhyme. Perhaps the sonnet is addressed to me; but I forget that he suppresses the affections! The only person in whom mamma takes much interest is the great French critic, M. Lejaune, whom we have the honour to carry with us. We have read a few of his works, though mamma disapproves of his tendencies and thinks him a dreadful materialist. We have read them for the style; you know he is one of the new Academicians. He is a Frenchman like any other, except that he is rather more quiet; and he has a gray mustache and the ribbon of the Legion of Honour. He is the first French writer of distinction who has been to America since De Tocqueville; the French, in such matters, are not very enterprising. Also, he has the air of wondering what he is doing *dans cette galère*. He has come with his *beau-frère*, who is an engineer, and is looking after some mines, and he talks with scarcely anyone else, as he speaks no English, and appears to take for granted that no one speaks French. Mamma would be delighted to assure him of the contrary; she has never conversed with an Academician. She always makes a little vague inclination, with a smile, when he passes her, and he answers with a most respectful bow; but it goes no farther, to mamma's disappointment. He is always with the *beau-frère*, a rather untidy, fat, bearded man – decorated, too, always smoking and looking at the feet of the ladies, whom mamma (though she has very good feet) has not the courage to *aborder*. I believe M. Lejaune is going to write a book about America, and Mr Leverett says it will be terrible. Mr Leverett has made his acquaintance, and says M. Lejaune will put him into his book; he says the movement of the French intellect is superb. As a general thing, he doesn't care for Academicians, but he thinks M. Lejaune is an exception, he is so living, so personal. I asked Mr Cockerel what he thought of M. Lejaune's plan of writing a book, and he answered that he didn't see what it mattered to him that a Frenchman the more should make a monkey of himself. I asked him why he hadn't written a book about Europe, and he said that, in the first place, Europe isn't worth writing about, and, in the second, if he said what he thought, people would think it was a joke. He said they are very superstitious about Europe over here; he wants people in America to behave as if Europe didn't exist. I told this to Mr Leverett, and he answered that if Europe didn't exist America wouldn't, for Europe keeps us alive by buying our corn. He said, also, that the trouble with America in the future will be that she will produce things in such enormous quantities that there won't be enough people in the rest of the world to buy them, and that we shall be left with our productions – most of them very hideous – on our hands. I asked him if he thought corn a hideous production, and he replied that there is nothing more unbeautiful than too much food. I think that to feed the world too well, however, that will be, after all, a *beau rôle*. Of course I don't understand these things, and I don't believe Mr Leverett does; but Mr Cockerel seems to know what he is talking about, and he says that America is complete in herself. I don't know exactly what he means, but he speaks as if human affairs had somehow moved over to this side of the world. It may be a very good place for them, and Heaven knows I am extremely tired of Europe, which mamma has always insisted so on my appreciating, but I don't think I like the idea of our being so completely cut off. Mr Cockerel says it is not we that are cut off, but Europe, and he seems to think that Europe has deserved it somehow. That may be; our life over there was sometimes extremely tiresome, though mamma says it is now that our real fatigues will begin. I like to abuse those dreadful old countries myself, but I am not sure that I am pleased when others do the same. We had some rather pretty moments there, after all; and at Piacenza we certainly lived on four francs a day. Mamma is already in a terrible state of mind about the expenses here; she is frightened by what people on the ship (the few that she has spoken to) have told her. There is one comfort, at any rate – we have spent so much money in coming here that we shall have none left to get away. I am scribbling along, as you see, to occupy me till we get news of the islands. Here comes Mr Cockerel to bring it. Yes, they are in sight; he tells me that they are lovelier than ever, and that I must come right up right away. I suppose you will think that I am already beginning to use the language of the country. It is certain that at the end of a month I shall speak nothing else. I have picked up every dialect, wherever we have travelled; you have heard my Platt-Deutsch and my Neapolitan. But, *voyons un peu* the Bay! I have just called to Mr Leverett to remind him of the islands. 'The islands – the islands? Ah, my dear young lady, I have seen Capri, I have seen Ischia!' Well, so have I, but that doesn't prevent… (A little later.) – I have seen the islands; they are rather queer.

MRS CHURCH, IN NEW YORK,
TO MADAME GALOPIN, AT GENEVA
October 17, 1880

If I felt far away from you in the middle of that deplorable Atlantic, *chère* Madame, how do I feel now, in the heart of this extraordinary city? We have arrived – we have arrived, dear friend; but I don't know whether to tell you that I consider that an advantage. If we had been given our choice of coming safely to land or going down to the bottom of the sea, I should doubtless have chosen the former course; for I hold, with your noble husband, and in opposition to the general tendency of modern thought, that our lives are not our own to dispose of, but a sacred trust from a higher power, by whom we shall be held responsible. Nevertheless, if I had foreseen more vividly some of the impressions that awaited me here, I am not sure that, for my daughter at least, I should not have preferred on the spot to hand in our account. Should I not have been less (rather than more) guilty in presuming to dispose of *her* destiny, than of my own? There is a nice point for dear M. Galopin to settle – one of those points which I have heard him discuss in the pulpit with such elevation. We are safe, however, as I say; by which I mean that we are physically safe. We have taken up the thread of our familiar pension-life, but under strikingly different conditions. We have found a refuge in a boarding house which has been highly recommended to me, and where the arrangements partake of that barbarous magnificence which in this country is the only alternative from primitive rudeness. The terms, per week, are as magnificent as all the rest. The landlady wears diamond earrings, and the drawing rooms are decorated with marble statues. I should indeed be sorry to let you know how I have allowed myself to be *rançonnée*; and I should be still more sorry that it should come to the ears of any of my good friends in Geneva, who know me less well than you and might judge me more harshly. There is no wine given for dinner, and I have vainly requested the person who conducts the establishment to garnish her table more liberally. She says I may have all the wine I want if I will order it at the merchant's, and settle the matter with him. But I have never, as you know, consented to regard our modest allowance of *eau rouge* as an extra; indeed, I remember that it is largely to your excellent advice that I have owed my habit of being firm on this point. There are, however, greater difficulties than the question of what we shall drink for dinner, *chère* Madame. Still, I have never lost courage, and I shall not lose courage now. At the worst, we can re-embark again, and seek repose and refreshment on the shores of your beautiful lake. (There is absolutely no scenery here!) We shall not, perhaps, in that case have achieved what we desired, but we shall at least have made an honourable retreat. What we desire – I know it is just this that puzzles you, dear friend; I don't think you ever really comprehended my motives in taking this formidable step, though you were good enough, and your magnanimous husband was good enough, to press my hand at parting in a way that seemed to say that you would still be with me, even if I was wrong. To be very brief, I wished to put an end to the reclamations of my daughter. Many Americans had assured her that she was wasting her youth in those historic lands which it was her privilege to see so intimately, and this unfortunate conviction had taken possession of her. 'Let me at least see for myself,' she used to say; 'if I should dislike it over there as much as you promise me, so much the better for you. In that case we will come back and make a new arrangement at Stuttgart.' The experiment is a terribly expensive one; but you know that my devotion never has shrunk from an ordeal. There is another point, moreover, which, from a mother to a mother, it would be affectation not to touch upon. I remember the just satisfaction with which you announced to me the betrothal of your charming Cécile. You know with what earnest care my Aurora has been educated – how thoroughly she is acquainted with the principal results of modern research. We have always studied together; we have always enjoyed together. It will perhaps surprise you to hear that she makes these very advantages a reproach to me, represents them as an injury to herself. 'In this country,' she says, 'the gentlemen have not those accomplishments, they care nothing for the results of modern research; and it will not help a young person to be sought in marriage that she can give an account of the last German theory of Pessimism.' That is possible; and I have never concealed from her that it was not for this country that I had educated her. If she marries in the United States it is, of course, my intention that my son-in-law shall accompany us to Europe. But, when she calls my attention more and more to these facts, I feel that we are moving in a different world. This is more and more the country of the many; the few find less and less place for them; and the individual – well, the individual has quite ceased to be recognised. He is recognised as a voter, but he is not recognised as a gentleman – still less as a lady. My daughter and I, of course, can only pretend to constitute a *few*! You know that I have never for a moment remitted my pretensions as an individual, though, among the agitations of pension-life, I have sometimes needed all my energy to uphold them. 'Oh, yes, I may be poor,' I have had occasion to say, 'I may be unprotected, I may be reserved, I may occupy a small apartment in the *quatrième*, and be unable to scatter unscrupulous bribes among the domestics; but at least I am a *person*, with personal rights.' In this country the people have rights, but the person has none. You would have perceived that if you had come with me to make arrangements at this establishment. The very fine lady who condescends to preside over it kept me waiting twenty minutes, and then came sailing in without a word of apology. I had sat very silent, with my eyes on the clock; Aurora amused herself with a false admiration of the room – a wonderful drawing room, with magenta curtains, frescoed walls, and photographs of the landlady's friends – as if one cared anything about her friends! When this exalted personage came in, she simply remarked that she had just been trying on a dress – that it took so long to get a skirt to hang. 'It seems to take very long indeed!' I answered. 'But I hope the skirt is right at last. You might have sent for us to come up and look at it!' She evidently didn't understand, and when I asked her to show us her rooms, she handed us over to a negro as *dégingandé* as herself. While we looked at them I heard her sit down to the piano in the drawing room; she began to sing an air from a comic opera. I began to fear we had gone quite astray; I didn't know in what house we could be, and was only reassured by seeing a Bible in every room. When we came down our musical hostess expressed no hope that the rooms had pleased us, and seemed quite indifferent to our taking them. She would not consent, moreover, to the least diminution, and was inflexible, as I told you, on the subject of wine. When I pushed this point, she was so good as to observe that she didn't keep a *cabaret*. One is not in the least considered; there is no respect for one's privacy, for one's preferences, for one's reserves. The familiarity is without limits, and I have already made a dozen acquaintances, of whom I know, and wish to know, nothing. Aurora tells me that she is the 'belle of the boarding house'. It appears that this is a great distinction. It brings me back to my poor child and her prospects. She takes a very critical view of them herself: she tells me that I have given her a false education, and that no one will marry her today. No American will marry her, because she is too much of a foreigner, and no foreigner will marry her because she is too much of an American. I remind her that scarcely a day passes that a foreigner, usually of distinction, doesn't select an American bride, and she answers me that in these cases the young lady is not married for her fine eyes. Not always, I reply; and then she declares that she would marry no foreigner who should not be one of the first of the first. You will say, doubtless, that she should content herself with advantages that have not been deemed insufficient for Cécile; but I will not repeat to you the remark she made when I once made use of this argument. You will doubtless be surprised to hear that I have ceased to argue; but it is time I should tell you that I have at last agreed to let her act for herself. She is to live for three months *à l'Américaine*, and I am to be a mere spectator. You will feel with me that this is a cruel position for a *coeur de mère*. I count the days till our three months are over, and I know that you will join with me in my prayers. Aurora walks the streets alone. She goes out in the tramway; a *voiture de place* costs five francs for the least little *course*. (I beseech you not to let it be known that I have sometimes had the weakness…) My daughter is sometimes accompanied by a gentleman – by a dozen gentlemen; she remains out for hours, and her conduct excites no surprise in this establishment. I know but too well the emotions it will excite in your quiet home. If you betray us, *chère* Madame, we are lost; and why, after all, should anyone know of these things in Geneva? Aurora pretends that she has been able to persuade herself that she doesn't care who knows them; but there is a strange expression in her face, which proves that her conscience is not at rest. I watch her, I let her go, but I sit with my hands clasped. There is a peculiar custom in this country – I shouldn't know how to express it in Genevese – it is called 'being attentive', and young girls are the object of the attention. It has not necessarily anything to do with projects of marriage – though it is the privilege only of the unmarried, and though, at the same time (fortunately, and this may surprise you), it has no relation to other projects. It is simply an invention by which young persons of the two sexes pass their time together. How shall I muster courage to tell you that Aurora is now engaged in this *délassement*, in company with several gentlemen? Though it has no relation to marriage, it happily does not exclude it, and marriages have been known to take place in consequence (or in spite) of it. It is true that even in this country a young lady may marry but one husband at a time, whereas she may receive at once the attentions of several gentlemen, who are equally entitled 'admirers'. My daughter, then, has admirers to an indefinite number. You will think I am joking, perhaps, when I tell you that I am unable to be exact – I who was formerly *l'exactitude même*. Two of these gentlemen are, to a certain extent, old friends, having been passengers on the steamer which carried us so far from you. One of them, still young, is typical of the American character, but a respectable person, and a lawyer in considerable practice. Everyone in this country follows a profession; but it must be admitted that the professions are more highly remunerated than *chez vous*. Mr Cockerel, even while I write you, is in complete possession of my daughter. He called for her an hour ago in a 'boghey' – a strange, unsafe, rickety vehicle, mounted on enormous wheels, which holds two persons very near together; and I watched her from the window take her place at his side. Then he whirled her away, behind two little horses with terribly thin legs; the whole equipage – and most of all her being in it – was in the most questionable taste. But she will return, and she will return very much as she went. It is the same when she goes down to Mr Louis Leverett, who has no vehicle, and who merely comes and sits with her in the front *salon*. He has lived a great deal in Europe, and is very fond of the arts, and though I am not sure I agree with him in his views of the relation of art to life and life to art, and in his interpretation of some of the great works that Aurora and I have studied together, he seems to me a sufficiently serious and intelligent young man. I do not regard him as intrinsically dangerous; but, on the other hand, he offers absolutely no guarantees. I have no means whatever of ascertaining his pecuniary situation. There is a vagueness on these points which is extremely embarrassing, and it never occurs to young men to offer you a reference. In Geneva I should not be at a loss; I should come to you, *chère* Madame, with my little enquiry, and what you should not be able to tell me would not be worth knowing. But no one in New York can give me the smallest information about the *état de fortune* of Mr Louis Leverett. It is true that he is a native of Boston, where most of his friends reside. I cannot, however, go to the expense of a journey to Boston simply to learn, perhaps, that Mr Leverett (the young Louis) has an income of five thousand francs. As I say, however, he does not strike me as dangerous. When Aurora comes back to me, after having passed an hour with the young Louis, she says that he has described to her his emotions on visiting the home of Shelley, or discussed some of the differences between the Boston Temperament and that of the Italians of the Renaissance. You will not enter into these *rapprochements*, and I can't blame you. But you won't betray me, *chère* Madame?

III
FROM MISS STURDY, AT NEWPORT,
TO MRS DRAPER, IN FLORENCE
September 30

I promised to tell you how I like it, but the truth is, I have gone to and fro so often that I have ceased to like and dislike. Nothing strikes me as unexpected; I expect everything in its order. Then, too, you know, I am not a critic; I have no talent for keen analysis, as the magazines say; I don't go into the reasons of things. It is true I have been for a longer time than usual on the wrong side of the water, and I admit that I feel a little out of training for American life. They are breaking me in very fast, however. I don't mean that they bully me; I absolutely decline to be bullied. I say what I think, because I believe that I have, on the whole, the advantage of knowing what I think – when I think anything – which is half the battle. Sometimes, indeed, I think nothing at all. They don't like that over here, they like you to have impressions. That they like these impressions to be favourable appears to me perfectly natural; I don't make a crime to them of that; it seems to me, on the contrary, a very amiable quality. When individuals have it, we call them sympathetic; I don't see why we shouldn't give nations the same benefit. But there are things I haven't the least desire to have an opinion about. The privilege of indifference is the dearest one we possess, and I hold that intelligent people are known by the way they exercise it. Life is full of rubbish, and we have at least our share of it over here. When you wake up in the morning you find that during the night a cartload has been deposited in your front garden. I decline, however, to have any of it in my premises; there are thousands of things I want to know nothing about. I have outlived the necessity of being hypocritical. I have nothing to gain and everything to lose. When one is fifty years old – single, stout, and red in the face – one has outlived a good many necessities. They tell me over here that my increase of weight is extremely marked, and though they don't tell me that I am coarse, I am sure they think me so. There is very little coarseness here – not quite enough, I think – though there is plenty of vulgarity, which is a very different thing. On the whole, the country is becoming much more agreeable. It isn't that the people are charming, for that they always were (the best of them, I mean, for it isn't true of the others), but that places and things as well have acquired the art of pleasing. The houses are extremely good, and they look so extraordinarily fresh and clean. European interiors, in comparison, seem musty and gritty. We have a great deal of taste; I shouldn't wonder if we should end by inventing something pretty; we only need a little time. Of course, as yet, it's all imitation, except, by the way, these piazzas. I am sitting on one now; I am writing to you with my portfolio on my knees. This broad light *loggia* surrounds the house with a movement as free as the expanded wings of a bird, and the wandering airs come up from the deep sea, which murmurs on the rocks at the end of the lawn. Newport is more charming even than you remember it; like everything else over here, it has improved. It is very exquisite today; it is, indeed, I think, in all the world, the only exquisite watering place, for I detest the whole genus. The crowd has left it now, which makes it all the better, though plenty of talkers remain in these large, light, luxurious houses, which are planted with a kind of Dutch definiteness all over the green carpet of the cliff. This carpet is very neatly laid and wonderfully well swept, and the sea, just at hand, is capable of prodigies of blue. Here and there a pretty woman strolls over one of the lawns, which all touch each other, you know, without hedges or fences; the light looks intense as it plays upon her brilliant dress; her large parasol shines like a silver dome. The long lines of the far shores are soft and pure, though they are places that one hasn't the least desire to visit. Altogether the effect is very delicate, and anything that is delicate counts immensely over here; for delicacy, I think, is as rare as coarseness. I am talking to you of the sea, however, without having told you a word of my voyage. It was very comfortable and amusing; I should like to take another next month. You know I am almost offensively well at sea – that I breast the weather and brave the storm. We had no storm fortunately, and I had brought with me a supply of light literature; so I passed nine days on deck in my sea-chair, with my heels up, reading Tauchnitz novels. There was a great lot of people, but no one in particular, save some fifty American girls. You know all about the American girl, however, having been one yourself. They are, on the whole, very nice, but fifty is too many; there are always too many. There was an enquiring Briton, a radical MP, by name Mr Antrobus, who entertained me as much as anyone else. He is an excellent man; I even asked him to come down here and spend a couple of days. He looked rather frightened, till I told him he shouldn't be alone with me, that the house was my brother's, and that I gave the invitation in his name. He came a week ago; he goes everywhere; we have heard of him in a dozen places. The English are very simple, or at least they seem so over here. Their old measurements and comparisons desert them; they don't know whether it's all a joke, or whether it's too serious by half. We are quicker than they, though we talk so much more slowly. We think fast, and yet we talk as deliberately as if we were speaking a foreign language. They toss off their sentences with an air of easy familiarity with the tongue, and yet they misunderstand two-thirds of what people say to them. Perhaps, after all, it is only *our* thoughts they think slowly; they think their own often to a lively tune enough. Mr Antrobus arrived here at eight o'clock in the morning; I don't know how he managed it; it appears to be his favourite hour; wherever we have heard of him he has come in with the dawn. In England he would arrive at 5.30 p.m. He asks innumerable questions, but they are easy to answer, for he has a sweet credulity. He made me rather ashamed; he is a better American than so many of us; he takes us more seriously than we take ourselves. He seems to think that an oligarchy of wealth is growing up here, and he advised me to be on my guard against it. I don't know exactly what I can do, but I promised him to look out. He is fearfully energetic; the energy of the people here is nothing to that of the inquiring Briton. If we should devote half the energy to building up our institutions that they devote to obtaining information about them, we should have a very satisfactory country. Mr Antrobus seemed to think very well of us, which surprised me, on the whole, because, say what one will, it's not so agreeable as England. It's very horrid that this should be; and it's delightful, when one thinks of it, that some things in England are, after all, so disagreeable. At the same time, Mr Antrobus appeared to be a good deal preoccupied with our dangers. I don't understand, quite, what they are; they seem to me so few, on a Newport piazza, on this bright, still day. But, after all, what one sees on a Newport piazza is not America; it's the back of Europe! I don't mean to say that I haven't noticed any dangers since my return; there are two or three that seem to me very serious, but they are not those that Mr Antrobus means. One, for instance, is that we shall cease to speak the English language, which I prefer so much to any other. It's less and less spoken; American is crowding it out. All the children speak American, and as a child's language it's dreadfully rough. It's exclusively in use in the schools; all the magazines and newspapers are in American. Of course, a people of fifty millions, who have invented a new civilisation, have a right to a language of their own; that's what they tell me, and I can't quarrel with it. But I wish they had made it as pretty as the mother-tongue, from which, after all, it is more or less derived. We ought to have invented something as noble as our country. They tell me it's more expressive, and yet some admirable things have been said in the Queen's English. There can be no question of the Queen over here, of course, and American no doubt is the music of the future. Poor dear future, how 'expressive' you'll be! For women and children, as I say, it strikes one as very rough; and, moreover, they don't speak it well, their own though it be. My little nephews, when I first came home, had not gone back to school, and it distressed me to see that, though they are charming children, they had the vocal inflections of little news-boys. My niece is sixteen years old; she has the sweetest nature possible; she is extremely well-bred, and is dressed to perfection. She chatters from morning till night; but it isn't a pleasant sound! These little persons are in the opposite case from so many English girls, who know how to speak, but don't know how to talk. My niece knows how to talk, but doesn't know how to speak. *A propos* of the young people, that is our other danger; the young people are eating us up – there is nothing in America but the young people. The country is made for the rising generation; life is arranged for them; they are the destruction of society. People talk of them, consider them, defer to them, bow down to them. They are always present, and whenever they are present there is an end to everything else. They are often very pretty; and, physically, they are wonderfully looked after; they are scoured and brushed, they wear hygienic clothes, they go every week to the dentist's. But the little boys kick your shins, and the little girls offer to slap your face! There is an immense literature entirely addressed to them, in which the kicking of shins and the slapping of faces is much recommended. As a woman of fifty, I protest. I insist on being judged by my peers. It's too late, however, for several millions of little feet are actively engaged in stamping out conversation, and I don't see how they can long fail to keep it under. The future is theirs; maturity will evidently be at an increasing discount. Longfellow wrote a charming little poem called 'The Children's Hour', but he ought to have called it 'The Children's Century'. And by children, of course, I don't mean simple infants; I mean everything of less than twenty. The social importance of the young American increases steadily up to that age, and then it suddenly stops. The young girls, of course, are more important than the lads; but the lads are very important too. I am struck with the way they are known and talked about; they are little celebrities; they have reputations and pretensions; they are taken very seriously. As for the young girls, as I said just now, there are too many. You will say, perhaps, that I am jealous of them, with my fifty years and my red face. I don't think so, because I don't suffer; my red face doesn't frighten people away, and I always find plenty of talkers. The young girls themselves, I believe, like me very much; and as for me, I delight in the young girls. They are often very pretty; not so pretty as people say in the magazines, but pretty enough. The magazines rather overdo that; they make a mistake. I have seen no great beauties, but the level of prettiness is high, and occasionally one sees a woman completely handsome. (As a general thing, a pretty person here means a person with a pretty face. The figure is rarely mentioned, though there are several good ones.) The level of prettiness is high, but the level of conversation is low; that's one of the signs of its being a young ladies' country. There are a good many things young ladies can't talk about; but think of all the things they can, when they are as clever as most of these. Perhaps one ought to content one's self with that measure, but it's difficult if one has lived for a while by a larger one. This one is decidedly narrow; I stretch it sometimes till it cracks. Then it is that they call me coarse, which I undoubtedly am, thank Heaven! People's talk is of course much more *châtiée* over here than in Europe; I am struck with that wherever I go. There are certain things that are never said at all, certain allusions that are never made. There are no light stories, no *propos risqués*. I don't know exactly what people talk about, for the supply of scandal is small, and it's poor in quality. They don't seem, however, to lack topics. The young girls are always there; they keep the gates of conversation; very little passes that is not inno-cent. I find we do very well without wickedness; and, for myself, as I take my ease, I don't miss my liberties. You remember what I thought of the tone of your table in Florence, and how surprised you were when I asked you why you allowed such things. You said they were like the courses of the seasons; one couldn't prevent them; also that to change the tone of your table you would have to change so many other things. Of course, in your house one never saw a young girl; I was the only spinster, and no one was afraid of me! Of course, too, if talk is more innocent in this country, manners are so, to begin with. The liberty of the young people is the strongest proof of it. The young girls are let loose in the world, and the world gets more good of it than *ces demoiselles* get harm. In your world – excuse me, but you know what I mean – this wouldn't do at all. Your world is a sad affair, and the young ladies would encounter all sorts of horrors. Over here, considering the way they knock about, they remain wonderfully simple, and the reason is that society protects them instead of setting them traps. There is almost no gallantry, as you understand it; the flirtations are child's play. People have no time for making love; the men, in particular, are extremely busy. I am told that sort of thing consumes hours; I have never had any time for it myself. If the leisure class should increase here considerably, there may possibly be a change; but I doubt it, for the women seem to me in all essentials exceedingly reserved. Great superficial frankness, but an extreme dread of complications. The men strike me as very good fellows. I think that at bottom they are better than the women, who are very subtle, but rather hard. They are not so nice to the men as the men are to them; I mean, of course, in proportion, you know. But women are not so nice as men 'anyhow', as they say here. The men, of course, are professional, commercial; there are very few gentlemen pure and simple. This personage needs to be very well done, however, to be of great utility; and I suppose you won't pretend that he is always well done in your countries. When he's not, the less of him the better. It's very much the same, however, with the system on which the young girls in this country are brought up. (You see, I have to come back to the young girls.) When it succeeds, they are the most charming possible; when it doesn't, the failure is disastrous. If a girl is a very nice girl, the American method brings her to great completeness – makes all her graces flower; but if she isn't nice, it makes her exceedingly disagreeable – elaborately and fatally perverts her. In a word, the American girl is rarely negative, and when she isn't a great success she is a great warning. In nineteen cases out of twenty, among the people who know how to live – I won't say what *their* proportion is – the results are highly satisfactory. The girls are not shy, but I don't know why they should be, for there is really nothing here to be afraid of. Manners are very gentle, very humane; the democratic system deprives people of weapons that everyone doesn't equally possess. No one is formidable; no one is on stilts; no one has great pretensions or any recognised right to be arrogant. I think there is not much wickedness, and there is certainly less cruelty than with you. Everyone can sit; no one is kept standing. One is much less liable to be snubbed, which you will say is a pity. I think it is to a certain extent; but, on the other hand, folly is less fatuous, in form, than in your countries; and as people generally have fewer revenges to take, there is less need of their being stamped on in advance. The general good nature, the social equality, deprive them of triumphs on the one hand, and of grievances on the other. There is extremely little impertinence; there is almost none. You will say I am describing a terrible society – a society without great figures or great social prizes. You have hit it, my dear: there are no great figures. (The great prize, of course, in Europe, is the opportunity to be a great figure.) You would miss these things a good deal – you who delight to contemplate greatness; and my advice to you, of course, is never to come back. You would miss the small people even more than the great; everyone is middle-sized, and you can never have that momentary sense of tallness which is so agreeable in Europe. There are no brilliant types; the most important people seem to lack dignity. They are very *bourgeois*; they make little jokes; on occasion they make puns; they have no form; they are too good-natured. The men have no style; the women, who are fidgety and talk too much, have it only in their *coiffure*, where they have it superabundantly. But I console myself with the greater *bonhomie*. Have you ever arrived at an English country house in the dusk of a winter's day? Have you ever made a call in London, when you knew nobody but the hostess? People here are more expressive, more demonstrative; and it is a pleasure, when one comes back (if one happens, like me, to be no one in particular), to feel one's social value rise. They attend to you more; they have you on their mind; they talk to you; they listen to you. That is, the men do; the women listen very little – not enough. They interrupt; they talk too much; one feels their presence too much as a sound. I imagine it is partly because their wits are quick, and they think of a good many things to say; not that they always say such wonders. Perfect repose, after all, is not *all* self-control; it is also partly stupidity. American women, however, make too many vague exclamations – say too many indefinite things. In short, they have a great deal of nature. On the whole, I find very little affectation, though we shall probably have more as we improve. As yet, people haven't the assurance that carries those things off; they know too much about each other. The trouble is that over here we have all been brought up together. You will think this a picture of a dreadfully insipid society;

but I hasten to add that it's not all so tame as that. I have been speaking of the people that one meets socially; and these are the smallest part of American life. The others – those one meets on a basis of mere convenience – are much more exciting; they keep one's temper in healthy exercise. I mean the people in the shops, and on the railroads; the servants, the hackmen, the labourers, everyone of whom you buy anything or have occasion to make an inquiry. With them you need all your best manners, for you must always have enough for two. If you think we are *too* democratic, taste a little of American life in these walks, and you will be reassured. This is the region of inequality, and you will find plenty of people to make your courtesy to. You see it from below – the weight of inequality is on your own back. You asked me to tell you about prices; they are simply dreadful.

IV

FROM THE HONOURABLE EDWARD ANTROBUS, MP, IN BOSTON, TO THE HONOURABLE MRS ANTROBUS
October 17

MY DEAR SUSAN – I sent you a postcard on the 13th and a native newspaper yesterday; I really have had no time to write. I sent you the newspaper partly because it contained a report – extremely incorrect – of some remarks I made at the meeting of the Association of the Teachers of New England; partly because it is so curious that I thought it would interest you and the children. I cut out some portions which I didn't think it would be well for the children to see; the parts remaining contain the most striking features. Please point out to the children the peculiar orthography, which probably will be adopted in England by the time they are grown up; the amusing oddities of expression, etc. Some of them are intentional; you will have heard of the celebrated American humour, etc. (remind me, by the way, on my return to Thistleton, to give you a few examples of it); others are unconscious, and are perhaps on that account the more diverting. Point out to the children the difference (in so far as you are sure that you yourself perceive it). You must excuse me if these lines are not very legible; I am writing them by the light of a railway lamp, which rattles above my left ear; it being only at odd moments that I can find time to look into everything that I wish to. You will say that this is a very odd moment, indeed, when I tell you that I am in bed in a sleeping-car. I occupy the upper berth (I will explain to you the arrangement when I return), while the lower forms the couch – the jolts are fearful – of an unknown female. You will be very anxious for my explanation; but I assure you that it is the custom of the country. I myself am assured that a lady may travel in this manner all over the Union (the Union of States) without a loss of consideration. In case of her occupying the upper berth I presume it would be different; but I must make inquiries on this point. Whether it be the fact that a mysterious being of another sex has retired to rest behind the same curtains, or whether it be the swing of the train, which rushes through the air with very much the same movement as the tail of a kite, the situation is, at any rate, so anomalous that I am unable to sleep. A ventilator is open just over my head, and a lively draught, mingled with a drizzle of cinders, pours in through this ingenious orifice. (I will describe to you its form on my return.) If I had occupied the lower berth I should have had a whole window to myself, and by drawing back the blind (a safe proceeding at the dead of night), I should have been able, by the light of an extraordinary brilliant moon, to see a little better what I write. The question occurs to me, however – would the lady below me in that case have ascended to the upper berth? (You know my old taste for contingent inquiries.) I incline to think (from what I have seen) that she would simply have requested me to evacuate my own couch. (The ladies in this country ask for anything they want.) In this case, I suppose, I should have had an extensive view of the country, which, from what I saw of it before I turned in (while the lady beneath me was going to bed), offered a rather ragged expanse, dotted with little white wooden houses, which looked in the moonshine like pasteboard boxes. I have been unable to ascertain as precisely as I should wish by whom these modest residences are occupied; for they are too small to be the homes of country gentlemen, there is no peasantry here, and (in New England, for all the corn comes from the far West) there are no yeomen nor farmers. The information that one receives in this country is apt to be rather conflicting, but I am determined to sift the mystery to the bottom. I have already noted down a multitude of facts bearing upon the points that interest me most – the operation of the school boards, the coeducation of the sexes, the elevation of the tone of the lower classes, the participation of the latter in political life. Political life, indeed, is almost wholly confined to the lower middle class, and the upper section of the lower class. In some of the large towns, indeed, the lowest order of all participates considerably – a very interesting phrase, to which I shall give more attention. It is very gratifying to see the taste for public affairs pervading so many social strata; but the indifference of the gentry is a fact not to be lightly considered. It may be objected, indeed, that there are no gentry; and it is very true that I have not yet encountered a character of the type of Lord Bottomley – a type which I am free to confess I should be sorry to see disappear from our English system, if system it may be called, where so much is the growth of blind and incoherent forces. It is nevertheless obvious that an idle and luxurious class exists in this country, and that it is less exempt than in our own from the reproach of preferring inglorious ease to the furtherance of liberal ideas. It is rapidly increasing, and I am not sure that the indefinite growth of the dilettante spirit, in connection with large and lavishly-expended wealth, is an unmixed good, even in a society in which freedom of development has obtained so many interesting triumphs. The fact that this body is not represented in the governing class, is perhaps as much the result of the jealousy with which it is viewed by the more earnest workers, as of its own – I dare not, perhaps, apply a harsher term than – levity. Such, at least, is the impression I have gathered in the Middle States and in New England. In the South-West, the North-West, and the far West, it will doubtless be liable to correction. These divisions are probably new to you; but they are the general denomination of large and flourish-ing communities, with which I hope to make myself at least superficially acquainted. The fatigue of traversing, as I habitually do, three or four hundred miles at a bound, is, of course, considerable; but there is usually much to inquire into by the way. The conductors of the trains, with whom I freely converse, are often men of vigorous and original minds, and even of some social eminence. One of them, a few days ago, gave me a letter of introduction to his brother-in-law, who is president of a Western University. Don't have any fear, therefore, that I am not in the best society! The arrangements for travelling are, as a general thing, extremely ingenious, as you will probably have inferred from what I told you above; but it must at the same time be conceded that some of them are more ingenious than happy. Some of the facilities, with regard to luggage, the transmission of parcels, etc., are doubtless very useful when explained, but I have not yet succeeded in mastering the intricacies. There are, on the other hand, no cabs and no porters, and I have calculated that I have myself carried my *impedimenta* – which, you know, are somewhat numerous, and from which I cannot bear to be separated – some seventy, or eighty miles. I have sometimes thought it was a great mistake not to bring Plummeridge; he would have been useful on such occasions. On the other hand, the startling question would have presented itself – who would have carried Plummeridge's portmanteau? He would have been useful, indeed, for brushing and packing my clothes, and getting me my tub; I travel with a large tin one – there are none to be obtained at the inns – and the transport of this receptacle often presents the most insoluble difficulties. It is often, too, an object of considerable embarrassment in arriving at private houses, where the servants have less reserve of manner than in England; and to tell you the truth, I am by no means certain at the present moment that the tub has been placed in the train with me. 'On board' the train is the consecrated phrase here; it is an allusion to the tossing and pitching of the concatenation of cars, so similar to that of a vessel in a storm. As I was about to inquire, however, who would get Plummeridge *his* tub, and attend to his little comforts? We could not very well make our appearance, on coming to stay with people, with *two* of the utensils I have named; though, as regards a single one, I have had the courage, as I may say, of a lifelong habit. It would hardly be expected that we should both use the same; though there have been occasions in my travels, as to which I see no way of blinking the fact, that Plummeridge would have had to sit down to dinner with me. Such a contingency would completely have unnerved him; and, on the whole, it was doubtless the wiser part to leave him respectfully touching his hat on the tender in the Mersey. No one touches his hat over here, and though it is doubtless the sign of a more advanced social order, I confess that when I see poor Plummeridge again, this familiar little gesture – familiar, I mean, only in the sense of being often seen – will give me a measurable satisfaction. You will see from what I tell you that democracy is not a mere word in this country, and I could give you many more instances of its universal reign. This, however, is what we come here to look at, and, in so far as there seems to be proper occasion, to admire; though I am by no means sure that we can hope to establish within an appreciable time a corresponding change in the somewhat rigid fabric of English manners. I am not even prepared to affirm that such a change is desirable; you know this is one of the points on which I do not as yet see my way to going as far as Lord B— . I have always held that there is a certain social ideal of inequality as well as of equality, and if I have found the people of this country, as a general thing, quite equal to each other, I am not sure that I am prepared to go so far as to say that, as a whole, they are equal to – excuse that dreadful blot! The movement of the train and the precarious nature of the light – it is close to my nose, and most offensive – would, I flatter myself, long since have got the better of a less resolute diarist! What I was not prepared for was the very considerable body of aristocratic feeling that lurks beneath this republican simplicity. I have on several occasions been made the confidant of these romantic but delusive vagaries, of which the stronghold appears to be the Empire City – a slang name for New York. I was assured in many quarters that that locality, at least, is ripe for a monarchy, and if one of the Queen's sons would come and talk it over, he would meet with the highest encouragement. This information was given me in strict confidence, with closed doors, as it were; it reminded me a good deal of the dreams of the old Jacobites, when they whispered their messages to the king across the water. I doubt, however, whether these less excusable visionaries will be able to secure the services of a Pretender, for I fear that in such a case he would encounter a still more fatal Culloden. I have given a good deal of time, as I told you, to the educational system, and have visited no fewer than one hundred and forty-three schools and colleges. It is extraordinary, the number of persons who are being educated in this country; and yet, at the same time, the tone of the people is less scholarly than one might expect. A lady, a few days since, described to me her daughter as being always 'on the go', which I take to be a jocular way of saying that the young lady was very fond of paying visits. Another person, the wife of a United States senator, informed me that if I should go to Washington in January, I should be quite 'in the swim'. I inquired the meaning of the phrase, but her explanation made it rather more than less ambiguous. To say that I am on the go describes very accurately my own situation. I went yesterday to the Pognanuc High School, to hear fifty-seven boys and girls recite in unison a most remarkable ode to the American flag, and shortly afterwards attended a ladies' lunch, at which some eighty or ninety of the sex were present. There was only one individual in trousers – his trousers, by the way, though he brought a dozen pairs, are getting rather seedy. The men in America do not partake of this meal, at which ladies assemble in large numbers to discuss religious, political and social topics. These immense female symposia (at which every delicacy is provided) are one of the most striking features of American life, and would seem to prove that men are not so indispensable in the scheme of creation as they sometimes suppose. I have been admitted on the footing of an Englishman – 'just to show you some of our bright women,' the hostess yesterday remarked. ('Bright' here has the meaning of *intellectual*.) I perceived, indeed, a great many intellectual foreheads. These curious collations are organised according to age. I have also been present as an inquiring stranger at several 'girls' lunches', from which married ladies are rigidly excluded, but where the fair revellers are equally numerous and equally bright. There is a good deal I should like to tell you about my study of the educational question, but my position is somewhat cramped, and I must dismiss it briefly. My leading impression is that the children in this country are better educated than the adults. The position of a child is, on the whole, one of great distinction. There is a popular ballad of which the refrain, if I am not mistaken, is 'Make me a child again, just for tonight!' and which seems to express the sentiment of regret for lost privileges. At all events they are a powerful and independent class, and have organs, of immense circulation, in the press. They are often extremely 'bright'. I have talked with a great many teachers, most of them lady-teachers, as they are called in this country. The phrase does not mean teachers of ladies, as you might suppose, but applies to the sex of the instructress, who often has large classes of young men under her control. I was lately introduced to a young woman of twenty-three, who occupies the chair of Moral Philosophy and Belles-Lettres in a Western college, and who told me with the utmost frankness that she was adored by the undergraduates. This young woman was the daughter of a petty trader in one of the South-Western states, and had studied at Amanda College, in Missourah, an institution at which young people of the two sexes pursue their education together. She was very pretty and modest, and expressed a great desire to see something of English country life, in consequence of which I made her promise to come down to Thistleton in the event of her crossing the Atlantic. She is not the least like Gwendolen or Charlotte, and I am not prepared to say how they would get on with her; the boys would probably do better. Still, I think her acquaintance would be of value to Miss Bumpus, and the two might pass their time very pleasantly in the schoolroom. I grant you freely that those I have seen here are much less comfortable than the schoolroom at Thistleton. Has Charlotte, by the way, designed any more texts for the walls? I have been extremely interested in my visit to Philadelphia, where I saw several thousand little red houses with white steps, occupied by intelligent artisans, and arranged (in streets) on the rectangular system. Improved cooking stoves, rosewood pianos, gas, and hot water, aesthetic furniture, and complete sets of the British Essayists. A tramway through every street; every block of equal length; blocks and houses scientifically lettered and numbered. There is absolutely no loss of time, and no need of looking for anything, or, indeed, at anything. The mind always on one's object; it is very delightful.

V

FROM LOUIS LEVERETT, IN BOSTON,
TO HARVARD TREMONT, IN PARIS
November

The scales have turned, my sympathetic Harvard, and the beam that has lifted you up has dropped me again on this terribly hard spot. I am extremely sorry to have missed you in London, but I received your little note, and took due heed of your injunction to let you know how I got on. I don't get on at all, my dear Harvard – I am consumed with the love of the farther shore. I have been so long away that I have dropped out of my place in this little Boston world, and the shallow tides of New England life have closed over it. I am a stranger here, and I find it hard to believe that I ever was a native. It is very hard, very cold, very vacant. I think of your warm, rich Paris; I think of the Boulevard St Michel on the mild spring evenings. I see the little corner by the window (of the Café de la Jeunesse) – where I used to sit; the doors are open, the soft deep breath of the great city comes in. It is brilliant, yet there is a kind of tone, of body, in the brightness; the mighty murmur of the ripest civilisation in the world comes in; the dear old *peuple de Paris*, the most interesting people in the world, pass by. I have a little book in my pocket; it is exquisitely printed, a modern Elzevir. It is a lyric cry from the heart of young France, and is full of the sentiment of form. There is no form here, dear Harvard; I had no idea how little form there was. I don't know what I shall do; I feel so undraped, so uncurtained, so uncushioned; I feel as if I were sitting in the centre of a mighty 'reflector'. A terrible crude glare is over everything; the earth looks peeled and excoriated; the raw heavens seem to bleed with the quick hard light. I have not got back my rooms in West Cedar Street; they are occupied by a mesmeric healer. I am staying at an hotel, and it is very dreadful. Nothing for one's self; nothing for one's preferences and habits. No one to receive you when you arrive; you push in through a crowd, you edge up to a counter; you write your name in a horrible book, where everyone may come and stare at it and finger it. A man behind the counter stares at you in silence. His stare seems to say to you, 'What the devil do *you* want?' But after this stare he never looks at you again. He tosses down a key at you; he presses a bell; a savage Irishman arrives. 'Take him away,' he seems to say to the Irishman; but it is all done in silence; there is no answer to your own speech – 'What is to be done with me, please?' 'Wait and you will see,' the awful silence seems to say. There is a great crowd around you, but there is also a great stillness; every now and then you hear someone expectorate. There are a thousand people in this huge and hideous structure; they feed together in a big white-walled room. It is lighted by a thousand gas jets, and heated by cast-iron screens, which vomit forth torrents of scorching air. The temperature is terrible; the atmosphere is more so; the furious light and heat seem to intensify the dreadful definiteness. When things are so ugly, they should not be so definite; and they are terribly ugly here. There is no mystery in the corners; there is no light and shade in the types. The people are haggard and joyless; they look as if they had no passions, no tastes, no senses. They sit feeding in silence, in the dry hard light; occasionally I hear the high firm note of a child. The servants are black and familiar; their faces shine as they shuffle about; there are blue tones in their dark masks. They have no manners; they address you, but they don't answer you; they plant themselves at your elbow (it rubs their clothes as you eat), and watch you as if your proceedings were strange. They deluge you with iced water; it's the only thing they will bring you; if you look round to summon them, they have gone for more. If you read the newspaper – which I don't, gracious Heaven! I can't – they hang over your shoulder and peruse it also. I always fold it up and present it to them; the newspapers here are indeed for an African taste. There are long corridors defended by gusts of hot air; down the middle swoops a pale little girl on parlour skates. 'Get out of my way!' she shrieks as she passes; she has ribbons in her hair and frills on her dress; she makes the tour of the immense hotel. I think of Puck, who put a girdle round the earth in forty minutes, and wonder what he said as he flitted by. A black waiter marches past me, bearing a tray, which he thrusts into my spine as he goes. It is laden with large white jugs; they tinkle as he moves, and I recognise the unconsoling fluid. We are dying of iced water, of hot air, of gas. I sit in my room thinking of these things – this room of mine which is a chamber of pain. The walls are white and bare, they shine in the rays of a horrible chandelier of imitation bronze, which depends from the middle of the ceiling. It flings a patch of shadow on a small table covered with white marble, of which the genial surface supports at the present moment the sheet of paper on which I address you; and when I go to bed (I like to read in bed, Harvard) it becomes an object of mockery and torment. It dangles at inaccessible heights; it stares me in the face; it flings the light upon the covers of my book, but not upon the page – the little French Elzevir that I love so well. I rise and put out the gas, and then my room becomes even lighter than before. Then a crude illumination from the hall, from the neighbouring room, pours through the glass openings that surmount the two doors of my apartment. It covers my bed, where I toss and groan. It beats in through my closed lids; it is accompanied by the most vulgar, though the most human, sounds. I spring up to call for some help, some remedy; but there is no bell, and I feel desolate and weak. There is only a strange orifice in the wall, through which the traveller in distress may transmit his appeal. I fill it with incoherent sounds, and sounds more incoherent yet come back to me. I gather at last their meaning; they appear to constitute a somewhat stern inquiry. A hollow impersonal voice wishes to know what I want, and the very question paralyses me. I want everything – yet I want nothing – nothing this hard impersonality can give! I want my little corner of Paris; I want the rich, the deep, the dark Old World; I want to be out of this horrible place. Yet I can't confide all this to that mechanical tube; it would be of no use; a mocking laugh would come up from the office. Fancy appealing in these sacred, these intimate moments, to an 'office'; fancy calling out into indifferent space for a candle, for a curtain! I pay incalculable sums in this dreadful house, and yet I haven't a servant to wait upon me. I fling myself back on my couch, and for a long time afterwards the orifice in the wall emits strange murmurs and rumblings. It seems unsatisfied, indignant; it is evidently scolding me for my vagueness. My vagueness, indeed, dear Harvard! I loathe their horrible arrangements; isn't that definite enough? You asked me to tell you whom I see, and what I think of my friends. I haven't very many. I don't feel at all *en rapport*. The people are very good, very serious, very devoted to their work; but there is a terrible absence of variety of type. Everyone is Mr Jones, Mr Brown; and everyone looks like Mr Jones and Mr Brown. They are thin; they are diluted in the great tepid bath of Democracy! They lack completeness of identity; they are quite without modelling. No, they are not beautiful, my poor Harvard; it must be whispered that they are not beautiful. You may say that they are as beautiful as the French, as the Germans; but I can't agree with you there. The French, the Germans, have the greatest beauty of all – the beauty of their ugliness – the beauty of the strange, the grotesque. These people are not even ugly; they are only plain. Many of the girls are pretty; but to be only pretty is (to my sense) to be plain. Yet I have had some talk. I have seen a woman. She was on the steamer, and I afterwards saw her in New York – a peculiar type, a real personality, a great deal of modelling, a great deal of colour, and yet a great deal of mystery. She was not, however, of this country; she was a compound of far-off things. But she was looking for something here – like me. We found each other, and for a moment that was enough. I have lost her now. I am sorry, because she liked to listen to me. She has passed away; I shall not see her again. She liked to listen to me; she almost understood!

VI
FROM M. GUSTAVE LEJAUNE, OF THE FRENCH ACADEMY,
TO M. ADOLPHE BOUCHE, IN PARIS
Washington, October 5

I give you my little notes; you must make allowances for haste, for bad inns, for the perpetual scramble, for ill-humour. Everywhere the same impression – the platitude of unbalanced democracy intensified by the platitude of the spirit of commerce. Everything on an immense scale – everything illustrated by millions of examples. My brother-in-law is always busy. He has appointments, inspections, interviews, disputes. The people, it appears, are incredibly sharp in conversation, in argument; they wait for you in silence at the corner of the road, and then they suddenly discharge their revolver. If you fall, they empty your pockets; the only chance is to shoot them first. With that, no amenities, no preliminaries, no manners, no care for the appearance. I wander about while my brother is occupied; I lounge along the streets; I stop at the corners; I look into the shops; *je regarde passer les femmes*. It's an easy country to see; one sees everything there is – the civilisation is skin deep; you don't have to dig. This positive, practical, pushing *bourgeoisie* is always about its business; it lives in the street, in the hotel, in the train; one is always in a crowd – there are seventy-five people in the tramway. They sit in your lap; they stand on your toes; when they wish to pass they simply push you. Everything in silence; they know that silence is golden, and they have the worship of gold. When the conductor wishes your fare he gives you a poke, very serious, without a word. As for the types – but there is only one – they are all variations of the same – the *commis-voyageur* minus the gaiety. The women are often pretty; you meet the young ones in the streets, in the trains, in search of a husband. They look at you frankly, coldly, judicially, to see if you will serve; but they don't want what you might think (*du moins on me l'assure*); they only want the husband. A Frenchman may mistake; he needs to be sure he is right, and I always make sure. They begin at fifteen; the mother sends them out; it lasts all day (with an interval for dinner at a pastry-cook's); sometimes it goes on for ten years. If they haven't found the husband then, they give it up; they make place for the *cadettes*, as the number of women is enormous. No *salons*, no society, no conversation; people don't receive at home; the young girls have to look for the husband where they can. It is no disgrace not to find him – several have never done so. They continue to go about unmarried – from the force of habit, from the love of movement, without hopes, without regret – no imagination, no sensibility, no desire for the convent. We have made several journeys – few of less than three hundred miles. Enormous trains, enormous *waggons*, with beds and lavatories, and negroes who brush you with a big broom, as if they were grooming a horse. A bounding movement, a roaring noise, a crowd of people who look horribly tired, a boy who passes up and down throwing pamphlets and sweetmeats into your lap – that is an American journey. There are windows in the *waggons* – enormous, like everything else; but there is nothing to see. The country is a void – no features, no objects, no details, nothing to show you that you are in one place more than another. *Aussi*, you are not in one place, you are everywhere, anywhere; the train goes a hundred miles an hour. The cities are all the same; little houses ten feet high, or else big ones two hundred; tramways, telegraph poles, enormous signs, holes in the pavement, oceans of mud, *commis-voyageurs*, young ladies looking for the husband. On the other hand, no beggars and no *cocottes* – none, at least, that you see. A colossal mediocrity, except (my brother-in-law tells me) in the machinery, which is magnificent. Naturally, no architecture (they make houses of wood and of iron), no art, no literature, no theatre. I have opened some of the books; *mais ils ne se laissent pas lire*. No form, no matter, no style, no general ideas! They seem to be written for children and young ladies. The most successful (those that they praise most) are the facetious; they sell in thousands of editions. I have looked into some of the most *vantés*; but you need to be forewarned, to know that they are amusing; *des plaisanteries de croquet-mort*. They have a novelist with pretensions to literature, who writes about the chase for the husband and the adventures of the rich Americans in our corrupt old Europe, where their primeval candour puts the Europeans to shame. *C'est proprement écrit*; but it's terribly pale. What isn't pale is the newspapers – enormous, like everything else (fifty columns of advertisements), and full of the *commérages* of a continent. And such a tone, *grand Dieu!* The amenities, the personalities, the recriminations, are like so many *coups de revolver*. Headings six inches tall; correspondences from places one never heard of; telegrams from Europe about Sarah Bernhardt; little paragraphs about nothing at all; the *menu* of the neighbour's dinner; articles on the European situation *à pouffer de rire*; all the *tripotage* of local politics. The *reportage* is incredible; I am chased up and down by the interviewers. The matrimonial infelicities of M. and Madame X (they give the name), *tout au long*, with every detail – not in six lines, discreetly veiled, with an art of insinuation, as with us; but with all the facts (or the fictions), the letters, the dates, the places, the hours. I open a paper at hazard, and I find *au beau milieu, à propos* of nothing, the announcement – 'Miss Susan Green has the longest nose in Western New York.' Miss Susan Green (*je me renseigne*) is a celebrated authoress; and the Americans have the reputation of spoiling their women. They spoil them *à coups de poing*. We have seen few interiors (no one speaks French); but if the newspapers give an idea of the domestic *moeurs*, the *moeurs* must be curious. The passport is abolished, but they have printed my *signalement* in these sheets – perhaps for the young ladies who look for the husband. We went one night to the theatre; the piece was French (they are the only ones), but the acting was American – too American. We came out in the middle. The want of taste is incredible. An Englishman whom I met tells me that even the language corrupts itself from day to day; an Englishman ceases to understand. It encourages me to find that I am not the only one. There are things every day that one can't describe. Such is Washington, where we arrived this morning, coming from Philadelphia. My brother-in-law wishes to see the Bureau of Patents, and on our arrival he went to look at his machines, while I walked about the streets and visited the Capitol! The human machine is what interests me most. I don't even care for the political – for that's what they call their Government here – 'the machine'. It operates very roughly, and some day, evidently, it will explode. It is true that you would never suspect that they have a government; this is the principal seat, but, save for three or four big buildings, most of them *affreux*, it looks like a settlement of negroes. No movement, no officials, no authority, no embodiment of the state. Enormous streets, *comme toujours*, lined with little red houses where nothing ever passes but the tramway. The Capitol – a vast structure, false classic, white marble, iron and stucco, which has *assez grand air* – must be seen to be appreciated. The goddess of liberty on the top, dressed in a bear's skin; their liberty over here is the liberty of bears. You go into the Capitol as you would into a railway station; you walk about as you would in the Palais Royal. No functionaries, no door-keepers, no officers, no uniforms, no badges, no restrictions, no authority – nothing but a crowd of shabby people circulating in a labyrinth of spittoons. We are too much governed, perhaps, in France; but at least we have a certain incarnation of the national conscience, of the national dignity. The dignity is absent here, and I am told that the conscience is an abyss. '*L'état c'est moi*' even – I like that better than the spittoons. These implements are architectural, monumental; they are the only monuments. *En somme*, the country is interesting, now that we too have the Republic; it is the biggest illustration, the biggest warning. It is the last word of democracy, and that word is – flatness. It is very big, very rich, and perfectly ugly. A Frenchman couldn't live here; for life with us, after all, at the worst is a sort of appreciation. Here, there is nothing to appreciate. As for the people, they are the English *minus* the conventions. You can fancy what remains. The women, *pourtant*, are sometimes rather well turned. There was one at Philadelphia – I made her acquaintance by accident – whom it is probable I shall see again.

She is not looking for the husband; she has already got one. It was at the hotel; I think the husband doesn't matter. A Frenchman, as I have said, may mistake, and he needs to be sure he is right. *Aussi*, I always make sure!

VII

FROM MARCELLUS COCKEREL, IN WASHINGTON, TO MRS COOLER, NÉE COCKEREL, AT OAKLAND, CALIFORNIA
October 25

I ought to have written to you long before this, for I have had your last excellent letter for four months in my hands. The first half of that time I was still in Europe; the last I have spent on my native soil. I think, therefore, my silence is owing to the fact that over there I was too miserable to write, and that here I have been too happy. I got back the 1st of September – you will have seen it in the papers. Delightful country, where one sees everything in the papers – the big, familiar, vulgar, good-natured, delightful papers, none of which has any reputation to keep up for anything but getting the news! I really think that has had as much to do as anything else with my satisfaction at getting home – the difference in what they call the 'tone of the press'. In Europe it's too dreary – the sapience, the solemnity, the false respectability, the verbosity, the long disquisitions on superannuated subjects. Here the newspapers are like the railroad trains, which carry everything that comes to the station, and have only the religion of punctuality. As a woman, however, you probably detest them; you think they are (the great word) vulgar. I admitted it just now, and I am very happy to have an early opportunity to announce to you that that idea has quite ceased to have any terrors for me. There are some conceptions to which the female mind can never rise. Vulgarity is a stupid, superficial, question-begging accusation, which has become today the easiest refuge of mediocrity. Better than anything else, it saves people the trouble of thinking, and anything which does that, succeeds. You must know that in these last three years in Europe I have become terribly vulgar myself; that's one service my travels have rendered me. By three years in Europe I mean three years in foreign parts altogether, for I spent several months of that time in Japan, India, and the rest of the East. Do you remember when you bade me goodbye in San Francisco, the night before I embarked for Yokohama? You foretold that I should take such a fancy to foreign life that America would never see me more, and that if *you* should wish to see me (an event you were good enough to regard as possible), you would have to make a rendezvous in Paris or in Rome. I think we made one (which you never kept), but I shall never make another for those cities. It was in Paris, however, that I got your letter; I remember the moment as well as if it were (to my honour) much more recent. You must know that, among many places I dislike, Paris carries the palm. I am bored to death there; it's the home of every humbug. The life is full of that false comfort which is worse than discomfort, and the small, fat, irritable people give me the shivers. I had been making these reflections even more devoutly than usual one very tiresome evening towards the beginning of last summer, when, as I re-entered my hotel at ten o'clock, the little reptile of a portress handed me your gracious lines. I was in a villainous humour. I had been having an overdressed dinner in a stuffy restaurant, and had gone from there to a suffocating theatre, where, by way of amusement, I saw a play in which blood and lies were the least of the horrors. The theatres over there are insupportable; the atmosphere is pestilential. People sit with their elbows in your sides; they squeeze past you every half-hour. It was one of my bad moments; I have a great many in Europe. The conventional perfunctory play, all in falsetto, which I seemed to have seen a thousand times; the horrible faces of the people; the pushing, bullying *ouvreuse*, with her false politeness, and her real rapacity, drove me out of the place at the end of an hour; and, as it was too early to go home, I sat down before a café on the Boulevard, where they served me a glass of sour, watery beer. There on the Boulevard, in the summer night, life itself was even uglier than the play, and it wouldn't do for me to tell you what I saw. Besides, I was sick of the Boulevard, with its eternal grimace, and the deadly sameness of the *article de Paris*, which pretends to be so various – the shop windows a wilderness of rubbish, and the passers-by a procession of manikins. Suddenly it came over me that I was supposed to be amusing myself – my face was a yard long – and that you probably at that moment were saying to your husband: 'He stays away so long! What a good time he must be having!' The idea was the first thing that had made me smile for a month; I got up and walked home, reflecting, as I went, that I was 'seeing Europe', and that, after all, one *must* see Europe. It was because I had been convinced of this that I came out, and it is because the operation has been brought to a close that I have been so happy for the last eight weeks. I was very conscientious about it, and, though your letter that night made me abominably homesick, I held out to the end, knowing it to be once for all. I sha'n't trouble Europe again; I shall see America for the rest of my days. My long delay has had the advantage that now, at least, I can give you my impressions – I don't mean of Europe; impressions of Europe are easy to get – but of this country, as it strikes the reinstated exile. Very likely you'll think them queer; but keep my letter, and twenty years hence they will be quite commonplace. They won't even be vulgar. It was very deliberate, my going round the world. I knew that one ought to see for one's self, and that I should have eternity, so to speak, to rest. I travelled energetically; I went everywhere and saw everything; took as many letters as possible, and made as many acquaintances. In short, I held my nose to the grindstone. The upshot of it all is that I have got rid of a superstition. We have so many, that one the less – perhaps the biggest of all – makes a real difference in one's comfort. The superstition in question – of course you have it – is that there is no salvation but through Europe. Our salvation is here, if we have eyes to see it, and the salvation of Europe into the bargain; that is, if Europe is to be saved, which I rather doubt. Of course you'll call me a bird of freedom, a braggart, a waver of the stars and stripes; but I'm in the delightful position of not minding in the least what anyone calls me. I haven't a mission; I don't want to preach; I have simply arrived at a state of mind; I have got Europe off my back. You have no idea how it simplifies things, and how jolly it makes me feel. Now I can live; now I can talk. If we wretched Americans could only say once for all, 'Oh, Europe be hanged!' we should attend much better to our proper business. We have simply to live our life, and the rest will look after itself. You will probably inquire what it is that I like better over here, and I will answer that it's simply – life. Disagreeables for disagreeables, I prefer our own. The way I have been bored and bullied in foreign parts, and the way I have had to say I found it pleasant! For a good while this appeared to be a sort of congenital obligation, but one fine day it occurred to me that there was no obligation at all, and that it would ease me immensely to admit to myself that (for me, at least) all those things had no importance. I mean the things they rub into you in Europe; the tiresome international topics, the petty politics, the stupid social customs, the baby-house scenery. The vastness and freshness of this American world, the great scale and great pace of our development, the good sense and good nature of the people, console me for there being no cathedrals and no Titians. I hear nothing about Prince Bismarck and Gambetta, about the Emperor William and the Czar of Russia, about Lord Beaconsfield and the Prince of Wales. I used to get so tired of their Mumbo-Jumbo of a Bismarck, of his secrets and surprises, his mysterious intentions and oracular words. They revile us for our party politics; but what are all the European jealousies and rivalries, their armaments and their wars, their rapacities and their mutual lies, but the intensity of the spirit of party? What question, what interest, what idea, what need of mankind, is involved in any of these things? Their big, pompous armies, drawn up in great silly rows, their gold lace, their salaams, their hierarchies, seem a pastime for children; there's a sense of humour and of reality over here that laughs at all that. Yes, we are nearer the reality – we are nearer what they will all have to come to. The questions of the future are social questions, which the Bismarcks and Beaconsfields are very much afraid to see settled; and the sight of a row of supercilious potentates holding their peoples like their personal property, and bristling all over, to make a mutual impression, with feathers and sabres, strikes us as a mixture of the grotesque and the abominable. What do we care for the mutual impressions of potentates who amuse themselves with sitting on people? Those things are their own affair, and they ought to be shut up in a dark room to have it out together. Once one feels, over here, that the great questions of the future are social questions, that a mighty tide is sweeping the world to democracy, and that this country is the biggest stage on which the drama can be enacted, the fashionable European topics seem petty and parochial.

They talk about things that we have settled ages ago, and the solemnity with which they propound to you their little domestic embarrassments makes a heavy draft on one's good nature. In England they were talking about the Hares and Rabbits Bill, about the extension of the County Franchise, about the Dissenters' Burials, about the Deceased Wife's Sister, about the abolition of the House of Lords, about heaven knows what ridiculous little measure for the propping-up of their ridiculous little country. And they call *us* provincial! It is hard to sit and look respectable while people discuss the utility of the House of Lords, and the beauty of a State Church, and it's only in a dowdy musty civilisation that you'll find them doing such things. The lightness and clearness of the social air, that's the great relief in these parts. The gentility of bishops, the propriety of parsons, even the impressiveness of a restored cathedral, give less of a charm to life than that. I used to be furious with the bishops and parsons, with the humbuggery of the whole affair, which everyone was conscious of, but which people agreed not to expose, because they would be compromised all round. The convenience of life over here, the quick and simple arrangements, the absence of the spirit of routine, are a blessed change from the stupid stiffness with which I struggled for two long years. There were people with swords and cockades, who used to order me about. For the simplest operation of life I had to kootoo to some bloated official. When it was a question of my doing a little differently from others, the bloated official gasped as if I had given him a blow on the stomach; he needed to take a week to think of it. On the other hand, it's impossible to take an American by surprise; he is ashamed to confess that he has not the wit to do a thing that another man has had the wit to think of. Besides being as good as his neighbour, he must therefore be as clever – which is an affliction only to people who are afraid he may be cleverer. If this general efficiency and spontaneity of the people – the union of the sense of freedom with the love of knowledge – isn't the very essence of a high civilisation, I don't know what a high civilisation is. I felt this greater ease on my first railroad journey – felt the blessing of sitting in a train where I could move about, where I could stretch my legs, and come and go, where I had a seat and a window to myself, where there were chairs, and tables, and food, and drink. The villainous little boxes on the

European trains, in which you are stuck down in a corner, with doubled-up knees, opposite to a row of people – often most offensive types, who stare at you for ten hours on end – these were part of my two years' ordeal. The large free way of doing things here is everywhere a pleasure. In London, at my hotel, they used to come to me on Saturday to make me order my Sunday's dinner, and when I asked for a sheet of paper, they put it into the bill. The meagreness, the stinginess, the perpetual expectation of a sixpence, used to exasperate me. Of course, I saw a great many people who were pleasant, but as I am writing to you, and not to one of them, I may say that they were dreadfully apt to be dull. The imagination among the people I see here is more flexible; and then they have the advantage of a larger horizon. It's not bounded on the north by the British aristocracy, and on the south by the *scrutin de liste*. (I mix up the countries a little, but they are not worth the keeping apart.) The absence of little conventional measurements, of little cut-and-dried judgements, is an immense refreshment. We are more analytic, more discriminating, more familiar with realities. As for manners, there are bad manners everywhere, but an aristocracy is bad manners organised. (I don't mean that they may not be polite among themselves, but they are rude to everyone else.) The sight of all these growing millions simply minding their business, is impressive to me – more so than all the gilt buttons and padded chests of the Old World; and there is a certain powerful type of 'practical' American (you'll find him chiefly in the West) who doesn't brag as I do (I'm not practical), but who quietly feels that he has the Future in his vitals – a type that strikes me more than any I met in your favourite countries. Of course you'll come back to the cathedrals and Titians, but there's a thought that helps one to do without them – the thought that though there's an immense deal of plainness, there's little misery, little squalor, little degradation. There is no regular wife-beating class, and there are none of the stultified peasants of whom it takes so many to make a European noble. The people here are more conscious of things. They invent, they act, they answer for themselves. They are not (I speak of social matters) tied up by authority and precedent. We shall have all the Titians by and by, and we shall move over a few cathedrals. You had better stay here if you want to have the best. Of course, I am a roaring Yankee, but you'll call me that if I say the least, so I may as well take my ease, and say the most. Washington's a most entertaining place, and here at least, at the seat of government, one isn't over-governed. In fact, there's no government at all to speak of; it seems too good to be true. The first day I was here I went to the Capitol, and it took me ever so long to figure to myself that I had as good a right there as anyone else – that the whole magnificent pile (it *is* magnificent, by the way) was in fact my own. In Europe one doesn't rise to such conceptions, and my spirit had been broken in Europe. The doors were gaping wide – I walked all about; there were no door-keepers, no officers, nor flunkeys – not even a policeman to be seen. It seemed strange not to see a uniform, if only as a patch of colour. But this isn't government by livery. The absence of these things is odd at first. You seem to miss something, to fancy the machine has stopped. It hasn't, though; it only works without fire and smoke. At the end of three days this simple negative impression – the fact is that there are no soldiers nor spies, nothing but plain black coats – begins to affect the imagination, becomes vivid, majestic, symbolic. It ends by being more impressive than the biggest review I saw in Germany. Of course, I'm a roaring Yankee; but one has to take a big brush to copy a big model. The future is here, of course; but it isn't only that – the present is here as well. You will complain that I don't give you any personal news; but I am more modest for myself than for my country. I spent a month in New York, and while I was there I saw a good deal of a rather interesting girl who came over with me in the steamer, and whom for a day or two I thought I should like to marry. But I shouldn't. She has been spoiled by Europe!

VIII
FROM MISS AURORA CHURCH, IN NEW YORK, TO MISS WHITESIDE, IN PARIS
January 9

I told you (after we landed) about my agreement with mamma – that I was to have my liberty for three months, and if at the end of this time I shouldn't have made a good use of it, I was to give it back to her.

Well, the time is up today, and I am very much afraid I haven't made a good use of it. In fact, I haven't made any use of it at all – I haven't got married, for that is what mamma meant by our little bargain. She has been trying to marry me in Europe, for years, without a *dot*, and as she has never (to the best of my knowledge) even come near it, she thought at last that, if she were to leave it to me, I might do better. I couldn't certainly do worse. Well, my dear, I have done very badly – that is, I haven't done at all. I haven't even tried. I had an idea that this affair came of itself over here; but it hasn't come to me. I won't say I am disappointed, for I haven't, on the whole, seen anyone I should like to marry. When you marry people over here, they expect you to love them, and I haven't seen anyone I should like to love. I don't know what the reason is, but they are none of them what I have thought of. It may be that I have thought of the impossible; and yet I have seen people in Europe whom I should have liked to marry. It is true, they were almost always married to someone else. What I *am* disappointed in is simply having to give back my liberty. I don't wish particularly to be married; and I do wish to do as I like – as I have been doing for the last month. All the same, I am sorry for poor mamma, as nothing has happened that she wished to happen. To begin with, we are not appreciated, not even by the Rucks, who have disappeared, in the strange way in which people over here seem to vanish from the world. We have made no sensation; my new dresses count for nothing (they all have better ones); our philological and historical studies don't show. We have been told we might do better in Boston; but, on the other hand, mamma hears that in Boston the people only marry their cousins. Then mamma is out of sorts because the country is exceedingly dear and we have spent all our money. Moreover, I have neither eloped, nor been insulted, nor been talked about, nor – so far as I know – deteriorated in manners or character; so that mamma is wrong in all her previsions. I think she would have rather liked me to be insulted. But I have been insulted as little as I have been adored. They don't adore you over here; they only make you think they are going to. Do you remember the two gentlemen who were on the ship, and who, after we arrived here, came to see me *à tour de rôle*? At first I never dreamed they were making love to me, though mamma was sure it must be that; then, as it went on a good while, I thought perhaps it *was* that; and I ended by seeing that it wasn't anything! It was simply conversation; they are very fond of conversation over here. Mr Leverett and Mr Cockerel disappeared one fine day, without the smallest pretension to having broken my heart, I am sure, though it only depended on me to think they had! All the gentlemen are like that; you can't tell what they mean; everything is very confused; society appears to consist of a sort of innocent jilting. I think, on the whole, I *am* a little disappointed – I don't mean about one's not marrying; I mean about the life generally. It seems so different at first, that you expect it will be very exciting; and then you find that, after all, when you have walked out for a week or two by yourself, and driven out with a gentleman in a buggy, that's about all there is of it, as they say here. Mamma is very angry at not finding more to dislike; she admitted yesterday that, once one has got a little settled, the country has not even the merit of being hateful. This has evidently something to do with her suddenly proposing three days ago that we should go to the West. Imagine my surprise at such an idea coming from mamma! The people in the *pension* – who, as usual, wish immensely to get rid of her – have talked to her about the West, and she has taken it up with a kind of desperation. You see, we must do something; we can't simply remain here. We are rapidly being ruined, and we are not – so to speak – getting married. Perhaps it will be easier in the West; at any rate, it will be cheaper, and the country will have the advantage of being more hate- ful. It is a question between that and returning to Europe, and for the moment mamma is balancing. I say nothing: I am really indifferent; perhaps I shall marry a pioneer. I am just thinking how I shall give back my liberty. It really won't be possible; I haven't got it any more; I have given it away to others. Mamma may recover it, if she can, from *them*! She comes in at this moment to say that we must push farther – she has decided for the West. Wonderful mamma! It appears that my real chance is for a pioneer – they have sometimes millions. But, fancy us in the West!

HESPERUS PRESS CLASSICS

Hesperus Press, as suggested by the Latin motto, is committed to bringing near what is far – far both in space and time. Works written by the greatest authors, and unjustly neglected or simply little known in the English-speaking world, are made accessible through new translations and a completely fresh editorial approach. Through these classic works, the reader is introduced to the greatest writers from all times and all cultures.

For more information on Hesperus Press, please visit our website: **www.hesperuspress.com**

ET REMOTISSIMA PROPE

BIOGRAPHICAL NOTE

Henry James, novelist, playwright, short-story writer and critic, was born in New York in 1843. Educated in France, Germany and Switzerland, he attended Harvard Law School in 1862, later travelling extensively across Europe – an experience that prompted his first published books: two volumes of travel essays in 1875. His first published novel, *Roderick Hudson*, appeared the following year, depicting an American's moral decline when in Rome, and relations between America and Europe formed the themes of further works, anticipating *The Portrait of a Lady* (1881).

From 1887, James lived in London, remaining there – his many European trips notwithstanding – until 1896, when he moved to Rye. His focus shifted to an exclusively English arena with his 1890 novel, *The Tragic Muse*, in which he explored the notion of the English character. He went on to pen biographies, literary criticism and the fragment of autobiography, *A Small Boy and Others* (1913), but in his later novels – *The Wings of the Dove* (1902), *The Ambassadors* (1903) and *The Golden Bowl* (1904) – he again returned to differences between America and Europe.

Today renowned as a master stylist whose novels often elaborate a moral consciousness torn between individual and social obligations, Henry James wrote with care and precision about Western civilisation as he understood it. Writing at a period when the novel form was reaching the heights of its sophistication, James critically examined the genre in his *The Art of Fiction* (1885), and praised Balzac above all other nineteenth-century novelists as 'the master of us all'. He assumed British nationality in 1915, dying the following year after suffering a stroke.